HEART'S DESIRE

DELANEY DIAMOND

GARDEN AVENUE PRESS

1

She pretended not to notice him, but that was nearly impossible. Nathan Crenshaw was hard to miss. He strode across the conference room floor with fluid movements, his walnut-brown skin practically glowing beneath the rays of the sun that came through the half-open blinds.

Today he wore all black—black slacks, jacket, tie, and a black shirt. Tall and muscular, he looked like one of the celebrities who frequented their high-end hotel, as if he'd left a photo shoot and stopped in for coffee. But Nathan could wear anything and look fashion-ready. She'd seen him lounging in sweats at his apartment, and he'd looked just as good.

Janice turned away, but the sound of his laughter cut through the low murmur of voices and made the hairs on the back of her neck stand up.

"Today he's wearing all black. Lord, that man is fine."

With her back turned to the room, Janice refrained from rolling her eyes at the breathless quality of Precious's voice.

Precious was Nathan's administrative assistant and didn't know that Janice and Nathan used to date. At work, no one did, because they'd kept their relationship hush-hush.

"Hello, ladies." His friendly voice floated on the air and filled the room.

Instead of turning around, Janice murmured a hello and ignored the quiver in her belly as she poured sugar into her post-lunch coffee.

"Hi, Nathan. How was your weekend?" Precious asked.

From the corner of her eye, Janice saw Precious straighten her spine and smooth her hands over her hips. If she weren't dark-skinned, a red blush would color her cheeks right now.

"Couldn't have been better. I took Abram to a basketball game, and his team won after a nail-biting finish in overtime. *And* he had the winning basket."

Nathan's sixteen-year-old brother played basketball in a community league organized by the churches in their area.

"That's wonderful!" Precious said, still breathless.

This time, Janice did roll her eyes as she stirred the sugar in her coffee.

"They're going to the finals. I'm really proud of him."

"I'm sure he's happy to have such a supportive big brother." Precious cleared her throat. "Did you get a chance to eat? I could order some food for you."

"No, I'm good. I grabbed a sandwich at the cafe downstairs."

"A sandwich? That's no good."

"It'll have to do. If I hadn't had that emergency conference call, I could have joined you all for lunch. I'm sure the food was delicious."

"It was. I love Italian. Too bad you missed it." Precious picked up her coffee. "I'll scoot on over to my seat and get in place to take notes. Excuse me."

As Nathan came to stand beside her at the sidebar, tension seeped into Janice's body.

"And how are you today, Janice?"

The way he said her name always did something to her. She rolled back her shoulders. "Great," she replied, calmly stirring cream in the coffee and then taking a tentative sip as she glanced sideways at him.

His dark brown skin was the perfect canvas for any color in the rainbow. Add to that his high cheekbones and lips as plump and succulent-looking as ripe plums, and it was no wonder he easily turned heads and had grown women crushing on him at work.

"And how was your weekend?" He poured a cup of coffee. He drank his with no sugar or cream, one of the many details she remembered from their relationship a few years ago.

"Nothing special."

"Did you go out?"

"I did. Went to a club and danced the night away. It was fun."

He slowly nodded. "Still partying hard, huh?"

"Not too hard." On occasion, she went to a club or lounge to relax on the weekend and unload the stress of the work week.

"I'm sure you had men lined up to be your dance partners."

"Nothing quite so dramatic," Janice demurred, though she was pleased by the compliment.

Nathan chuckled, low and sexy, showing off pretty teeth and dimples. She hated that laugh. Not because it annoyed her, but because it was so enticing she longed to hear it over and over again and highlighted the smallest regret that she and Nathan were no longer a couple.

But they were in a good place now, and she had to remember that. Friendly, able to engage in polite conversation and the occasional banter the way they used to before they became romantically involved.

"At least you're not still wasting your time with boys," he said, amusement filtering into his eyes.

Janice arched an eyebrow. "Who says I'm wasting my time with boys?"

"I've seen the men you date now, remember?" He lowered his voice, arching an eyebrow right back at her.

Janice's voice also went lower. "*Once*. One time you saw me on a date with a younger man. That's not my norm." Unfortunately, she'd run into Nathan at the movie theater she and her date had gone to.

At thirty-six, she figured she'd try something different, so why not try a younger man? She'd assumed younger men were easier to deal with in relationships, and she wouldn't have to worry about getting serious because they were in their prime and not looking for anything permanent. *Au contraire.* Her experiment had been a bust. The first one she dated was too immature and saw her as a bank to borrow money from. The second became attached way too soon, so she'd had to end the relationship before it started.

"You shouldn't waste time with boys when you could have the benefits of being with a real man."

"And I suppose you can tell me all about the benefits of being with a real man?" Janice asked sweetly. They were entering dangerous territory.

Nathan locked eyes with her, seemed about to add more, and then shook his head. After a few seconds, he said, "I'm not going there."

"Say what's on your mind," Janice said, her heart rate speeding up a fraction.

"Nah. Not a good idea." His gaze swept the room as if searching for someone.

"Tell me before I beat it out of you."

His attention came back to her. For a second, he hesitated, but then he finally whispered, "I can show you all the benefits of being with a real man better than I can tell you. But you already know that."

They locked eyes again, and her stomach tightened.

Janice swallowed. "You did, but that didn't work so well, did it?"

"So you say." Nathan sipped his coffee and then his long-limbed body strolled across the carpeted floor and engaged a male member of the staff in conversation.

Janice released a quiet breath and propped her weight against the counter. The edge dug into her lower back, but she barely registered the pain. The tension that always surfaced whenever she came into close proximity to Nathan slowly oozed from her body. Being around him had always made her behave that way—like a weak-kneed high-schooler with a crush on the most popular boy.

When they first started working together, Janice hadn't really paid attention to the mild attraction she felt for him. At the time, he wasn't her supervisor, like he was now. She wasn't blind, but she'd had no intention of acting on her attraction to a coworker.

Then one night they worked late on a project and afterward stayed in his office, drinking Scotch from the mini-bar and talking on his couch, both of them obviously loathe to leave since they were enjoying themselves so much. She opened up to him in a way she hadn't to anyone else but her closest friends. They shared stories about past relationships, doubling over with laughter at some of the drama they'd both experienced.

When he finally walked her to the car, the buzz of the alcohol they'd drunk and the intimate, casual conversation made her hyperaware of his sexual appeal. At one point they stopped laughing, their gazes met, and when Nathan leaned in, Janice leaned in too.

The kiss had been electrifying. Toe-curling. They made it as far as the back seat of her car, where he pulled her onto his lap. She ground her pelvis against him and pushed her tongue into his mouth. His fingers climbed into her curly hair, tightening as he fastened her mouth to his.

That was the first night they'd had sex, and the next thing Janice knew, she was in a relationship. Six months later, they broke up when she volunteered for a transfer to the California office for a temporary gig to get the staff over there straightened out.

She was only supposed to be in California for six months, but it turned into two years before she transferred back nine months ago.

In the interim, he received the promotion to vice-president of finance. Somehow, they'd segued back into a cool work friendship, but time and distance hadn't quelled her feelings for him. Especially when he was prone to making occasional remarks that made her wonder about what could have been. She completely ignored the warmth in her belly whenever he stood close and pretended that she didn't look forward to seeing him every day and wasn't disappointed when he didn't come into the office because of travel.

She was really, really good at pretending. Occasionally his comments—like the one he made about giving her lessons again—made pretending harder. She simply needed to remember what happened the last time she met a man as slick as Nathan. A man who, like Nathan, came across as thoughtful and considerate and wrapped in a too-perfect package. She'd experienced a broken engagement and a broken heart to go along with it. No way was she going to let Nathan put her through that type of emotional turmoil again.

No matter how appealing his personality and enticing his good looks.

DAMN. He had to control his tongue when he was around

Janice. His comment was completely inappropriate for a VP of a multimillion-dollar company. Not to mention he wasn't in a position to talk to Janice—or any woman, for that matter—in that way. He was in a serious relationship.

Nathan excused himself from the conversation with one of the regional vice-presidents and went to the front of the room. Looking out at the staff, some standing, others sitting, he smiled and asked, "How was lunch, everyone?"

Murmurs of "Great" and "Thanks" filled the room.

"Sorry I couldn't join you, but duty called. You know how it is."

Everyone laughed.

"I'm glad you enjoyed yourself anyway, but we all know the next few days are not only about leisure. Our semi-annual meeting is a time for us to congratulate you on a job well done over the past six months, but also to discuss policy and objectives."

"Of course," the accounting director said dryly, and laughter filled the room.

Nathan pointed at him. "Don't start, William."

More laughter.

"Anyway, I'll let David take over with the presentation, and when he's finished, I'll add a few words."

Nathan went to stand at the back of the room and pretended to pay attention to what the regional vice-president for the Midwest was saying, but his eyes followed Janice's progression to the table, mug in hand. She had squeezed her ripe, lush body into an orange figure-hugging dress and wore reading glasses in the same bright orange. She changed glasses like she did accessories, and he'd lost track of how many different colored frames she owned.

The nine months since her return from California had been problematic to his peace of mind, to say the least. He'd dated other women during that period and found someone he intended to spend the rest of his life with, yet he constantly wondered about what could have been with Janice. A couple of years ago, he'd almost gone crazy when she pointed out their relationship wouldn't work because of the distance, and then left. She'd behaved as if what they'd shared hadn't been as earth-shattering for her as it had been for him.

Nathan broodingly sipped his coffee and smiled politely when laughter filled the room. He had no idea what David had said, too busy watching Janice. Her dress made her hard to miss in the sea of gray, blue, and black, and she wore a ton of colorful bangles on her wrists. Then there was her hair—red corkscrew curls covered her head and kissed her shoulders. With bronze skin and curvaceous lips, she could easily stop traffic. But that's not why he'd fallen for her years ago. It was because of, quite frankly, her personality.

Janice was the friendly type who never met a stranger. She was easy to talk to, and they had a lot in common. They liked the same shows, and both liked to go jogging or motorcycle-riding on the weekends. Add in a quirky, outgoing personality, and as far as he was concerned, she had been the perfect girl-friend during those six months. He would have continued seeing her long-distance if she'd allowed it. But she hadn't, and he hadn't forgotten the words she said before she left. *This isn't going to work.*

Bullshit. She hadn't even tried.

But what could he do? And what could he do now? She'd moved on, and he planned to do the same.

2

"I have bad news and worse news," Nathan said.

He sat on the corner of his desk in a long-sleeved white shirt and black pants. The clothes fit him perfectly, the shirt showing off a hint of his biceps, while his thick thigh muscles pressed into the fabric of the pants.

Janice made that quick assessment without staring. Being around Nathan was a daily battle of not trying to jump his bones, one she fought valiantly and had so far won.

He'd called her into his office for a quick meeting, but the expression on his face let her know he was exasperated.

"Bad news?"

She sat in one of the black chairs. He preferred grays and black, and he'd chosen those neutral colors to decorate his office. She found the monochromatic color scheme boring and unstimulating. It was perhaps the most significant difference between them.

"The emergency phone call I had to address on Monday—the call which made me late to the lunch—is based on this right here." Nathan extended a blue folder, and she took it.

She crossed her legs, glancing up in time to catch him

watch the movement with what could only be described as a look of hunger that produced an answering ache in the middle of her thighs. He quickly masked the expression and went over to the mini-bar in his office.

That look had caught her by surprise. They didn't spend much time together. There was no reason to, preferring to let their assistants handle most of the communication between them. By silent, mutual agreement, they'd chosen this method to alleviate any unnecessary awkwardness. Right then, she experienced more than awkwardness. She felt a surge of feminine power and surprise that she could maybe still affect him in some way.

Janice perused the typewritten pages in the folder. "What am I looking at?"

"The next big project handed down from the president. Can I get you anything to drink?"

"No, thanks. So this was the emergency?" she asked.

Nathan nodded and came back over to the desk, a can of soda in his hand. "Our wonderful president forgot all about it and dropped this in my lap on her way out of the country to her vacation. Word is, The Heir is moving back to the States, and she has very specific ideas about what she wants to have done."

Nina Winthrop was the sole owner of The Winthrop Hotel Group, inherited from her father after his death. She was often referred to as The Heir, which could be used in a derogatory way, depending on the speaker.

Nina was a young woman who didn't spend much time participating in the hotel business at all. In fact, she had been overseas for much of the past couple of years, volunteering her time and donating dollars in other parts of the world. Apparently, she'd forwarded changes she wanted to implement upon her return to the United States.

Nathan continued speaking. "That's our new plan of action. She wants to create a new position—Head of Volunteerism, or something like that—title to be determined. It might be an executive-level post, from what I understand."

Janice raised her eyebrows. It was unusual to see someone in Nina's position so dedicated to helping others. "She's serious about this."

"It appears so. Anyway, she wants us to roll out a plan to get the staff more involved in volunteering. Now for the worse news. Can you guess which region she wants to start the testing in?"

"The east coast?"

"How'd you figure that out?" Nathan flashed a pretty, white-toothed smile.

As the regional vice-president of finance for The Winthrop Group's east coast hotels, the project was solidly her responsibility.

Janice groaned, under the guise of annoyance at the new project, but in reality, she made the sound because he had one of the prettiest smiles she'd ever seen. It reminded her of all the nasty things he'd do to her in bed, and then chuckle and smile in a self-satisfied way while she came down off a sexual high. He was fair and decent at work, but inappropriate and dirty in bed. The perfect man.

It was incredibly generous that a multimillionaire like Nina Winthrop was concerned about people not so fortunate, but her Pollyanna views could become a thorn in Janice's side and had proven problematic to other members of the executive team. The president didn't care for her and often complained about the absentee heir, pointing out that they were more concerned about making sure the company turned a profit than she was.

Reviewing the documents, Janice noted how the president planned to roll out the new program, where employees would be compensated for volunteer work.

"This is very ambitious. Is it realistic?" She lifted her gaze from the papers.

"That's what we're supposed to determine. Operations and finance are to work hand-in-hand to make Ms. Winthrop's vision a reality. We have to keep track of the numbers to see how much the program affects the bottom line, operations will make sure we're not short-staffed, and also determine how this affects staff morale and productivity in general. At the end of the trial period, we should be able to recommend whether the volunteerism idea should be implemented throughout the company."

"I need this project like I need a hole in the head," Janice muttered.

"You and me both, but it's coming from the top."

"I guess we have to keep her happy since she controls the money."

"She's young and not a bad person. Maybe a bit idealistic."

"You've met her?"

"Once. She's kind of laid-back. Not in the least bit flamboyant. You wouldn't know she was a millionaire. Of course, that doesn't matter to our president. She hates when Ms. Winthrop gets these ideas and can't understand why her advisors don't talk her out of them."

"They're probably yes-men and women, too afraid to say anything contrary to what the owner wants. Meanwhile, we have to execute these plans. Anything else I should know?"

"There are a few more points I need to go over with you."

They discussed additional details, and Janice had a few questions before the meeting ended. Then she stood.

"I'll walk you out." Nathan removed his jacket from the back of the leather executive chair, and as he shoved his arms through the sleeves, fell into step beside her.

"Headed to a meeting?"

"No. Out to an early lunch." He opened the door so she could walk ahead of him.

"You're going really early. By over an hour."

"I have to take care of something that I've put off long enough. I figured I'll take a couple of hours and do what I need to do." Straightening his lapels, he avoided eye contact. At least, that's what she felt he was doing—avoiding eye contact. But why?

At the elevator, she said, "I'll get to work on this, and I'll see you later."

Nathan nodded and then stepped between the open doors.

3

C *rap.*

Janice stared in dismay at the flat tire on the back passenger's side of her custom-painted mint-green Avalon. After a long day, it was the last thing she wanted to see.

Scanning the covered parking deck, she saw very few cars, but one of them happened to be Nathan's electric-blue Mercedes SUV. An interesting choice for a man who preferred neutral colors.

She mentally kicked herself for putting off scheduling classes at the mechanic clinic that specifically taught women how to maintain and perform minor repairs to their cars. Had she gone, she would know what to do right now.

She wasn't the handy type, but how hard could it be to change a tire? All she had to do was take off the old tire and put on a new one. There were probably tons of YouTube videos she could consult for help.

"Or call roadside assistance!" she said with sudden excitement.

Janice pulled out her phone and tossed her purse onto the leather seat. She was about to dial the 800 number when she paused. She could call, but they probably wouldn't get help to her for over an hour. Exhausted and ready to go home, did she really want to wait that long?

No, she didn't.

She glanced again at Nathan's SUV. He'd help her if she asked because he was that kind of man. The question was, should she ask? Was it appropriate to ask your ex and current supervisor, whom you barely talked to at length outside of work matters, to change your car tire?

Apparently so, because she dialed Nathan's direct line in the office.

When he answered, she infused extra cheeriness into her voice. "Hey, Nathan!"

Pause. "Hey," he replied more slowly, cautiously.

Janice nervously twirled a lock of hair as she talked. "Um, are you busy? I need a big favor."

"I'm wrapping up some reports before I leave the office. What do you need?" She heard shuffling papers as he spoke.

Relieved that he didn't seem disinclined to assist her, Janice answered, "I'm downstairs in the parking deck and need your help. I have a completely flat tire, and...I was wondering if you'd mind..." She bit the corner of her bottom lip.

"Huh. So you never learned to change a flat tire even though I told you it was an important skill to learn? I told you that years ago, Janice."

"Yes, you did, and you were right that I should have learned to do that by now. Happy?" She couldn't help smiling even as her voice dripped with sarcasm.

"Immensely." Amusement also colored his voice. "Let me finish up here. It shouldn't take more than another two minutes, and then I'll be down."

"Thank you," she said.

She knew he'd come. Nathan's generous heart had at one

time been a bone of contention between them because his helpfulness had extended to one of his exes.

While she'd anticipated he'd help, she hadn't expected the level of excitement she'd feel that he was coming. They saw each other almost every day at work because their offices were in the same department on the same floor, but their interactions were restricted to work-related issues.

This was the first time in a long time that they would spend time together outside of the building, and the thought of that sent adrenaline surging in her veins.

Five minutes later, Nathan's commanding stride carried him from the elevator to her side. Today he wore a black suit with a burgundy shirt and skinny black tie. Conservative and typical and nothing but sexy.

"No gloating," she said, as her heart skipped a little faster.

"I never gloat."

"We both know that's a lie."

Nothing made him happier than being right, and that was because he always strived for perfection in every part of his life.

"I'll ignore that since you clearly don't know the proper etiquette for greeting someone who's trying to help you."

"Ouch. Point made." She smiled sweetly at him, and he smiled back.

Their gazes lingered for a little too long, sending heat crawling up her neck. She was the first to break eye contact, clearing her throat and making a big show of pointing out the flat tire.

Nathan removed his jacket, and she took it from him. After a long day at work, the expensive fabric carried the scent of his cologne and the natural smell of his body. She almost lost the battle to press her nose to the material and take a deep drag.

Her chest grew warm, and her inner thighs throbbed at the memory of them leaving a movie theater late one night when they were dating. The temperature had dropped during the hours they were inside, and despite wearing a cardigan, she shivered in the cold air.

Nathan had draped his jacket over her shoulders for the walk to the car. She'd been so turned on by the smell of him that she practically tore off his clothes when they arrived at her apartment.

She also remembered how the scent of him stayed in her bed after he'd slept there all night. During those months together, how many times had she rolled over—somewhere between sleep and awake—and slid a smooth thigh between his hair-sprinkled ones, then pressed her nose to his neck to revel in his male scent? Nothing smelled better than a fragrant man, especially when the man was wrapped in a body as fine as Nathan's.

The truth was, after three years, she still missed him, and at times the ache in her chest felt as deep as a crater. She longed to be close to him again—to fix the mess she created, but didn't know how.

Nathan crouched beside the wheel and flung his tie over one shoulder as he examined the damage.

"I don't know how that happened. Maybe I ran over a nail."

Nathan stood. "Maybe. Anyplace in particular you could have picked it up?"

"I don't know if you know this, but I bought a foreclosure, and I'm having it renovated."

Nathan's eyebrows lifted in surprise. "I didn't know that. Pop the trunk." He walked to the back of the car.

Janice did as he asked and continued talking. "Anyway, I went by the house this afternoon during my lunch break to see about a wall the contractor told me he couldn't move as planned. According to him, it's a load-bearing wall, so we decided that instead of removing it completely to open the room, we'll turn it into an arched entryway from the kitchen into the den."

"Nice compromise."

"I do like the idea better than simply opening up the space between the rooms. Anyway, I said all that to say that I believe that's where I picked up the nail."

"That's very possible." Nathan deposited the spare tire, an L-shaped lug wrench, and the jack near the back of the vehicle.

"Can I help with anything?" Janice asked.

Nathan smiled faintly. "If you had learned how to do this, I wouldn't be here. So no, you can't help."

"You couldn't resist, could you?"

"I'm allowed to gloat a little." The smile widened and put his dimples on display.

Janice's stomach tightened. "A little," she said softly, too softly as her whole face flushed with heat.

Nathan tugged off his tie and opened the top button of his shirt. He handed the tie to Janice and then rolled up his sleeves. He'd done all that to get more comfortable, but he was slowly killing her with his casual sex appeal.

His rolled-up sleeves exposed veined, muscular forearms, the left one covered in tattoos which she knew from experience extended all the way up to the base of his neck.

Conservative, dependable Nathan had gone through a rebellious phase at one time. She'd known from casual observation in the office that he had tattoos, but she'd never forgotten the first time she saw the full extent of the colorful ink on his body. It had been the night they first hooked up, and the artwork had turned her on even more than she already had been.

Tattoos were pretty commonplace. She had a couple herself —*love is a gift* on the inside of her left wrist, and the same words written in Swahili on her right ankle. But seeing the ink on Nathan gave him an unexpected edginess and suggested that square Nathan wasn't so square after all. Seeing another side of his persona drew her the way a weary traveler was drawn to a desert oasis.

As he jacked up the vehicle, she stepped back and watched him work. When the tire was well off the ground, he examined it and found the puncture point.

"Nail," he said, tapping the spot where it was embedded in the rubber.

"So I probably did get it from going to the house."

"Could have been anywhere, but I'd say that's a good guess."

"I have to be more careful when I go there in the future."

"When will the renovations be finished?"

She let out a dry laugh. "They were supposed to be finished two months ago. I know the place will be gorgeous when it's done, but I'm so anxious about all the details."

"Patience is not one of your strong suits," Nathan said dryly.

"Please keep all negative comments to yourself."

He laughed softly and began removing the lug nuts. "You'll be able to get home on this donut, but it's not designed to last very long. You'll need to get a normal-sized tire as soon as possible, okay?"

"Okay." *How soon is soon,* she wondered.

As if he read her mind, Nathan said, "Go to the mechanic first thing tomorrow before you come into work. I'm giving you permission to come in late. And by the way, these tires are not meant to be driven on fast."

"Fast as in—"

"Fast as in don't go over fifty miles per hour. I know driving slower will be hard for you, but you have to do it." The tone of his voice sent a thrill through her.

He talked while he worked, glancing up at her every now and again, his voice firm in the way that it became whenever he was in a commanding mood in bed. During those moments, his hands became firmer too, and his voice became lower, deeper, almost a growl in her ear.

Come here.

You like that, don't you?

Janice took a cleansing breath and paced away.

"Calm down," she muttered to herself.

"What did you say?" Nathan asked over his shoulder.

"Nothing." She couldn't possibly answer him truthfully. "For the record, I know when to go slow. Don't worry, I'll do as you command."

For a split second, Nathan froze. Then he resumed removing the last nut. She wouldn't have noticed except she was looking right at him. Tension filled the air as she became even more aware of him, and the words of the last sentence replayed in her mind. Did he feel it, too?

I'll do as you command.

The statement was supposed to be sarcastic, a way to tease him and alleviate some of the sexual energy that surrounded her in his presence. Her words had the opposite effect.

Her gaze swept over Nathan's long fingers and dwelled on the tension in his muscles as he used the wrench to remove the final bolt.

She was definitely accustomed to doing as he said.

Open for me.

Lift those hips. That's it.

Where was a bucket of ice water when you needed one?

4

"You still take the Harley out?" Nathan asked.

"I haven't taken it out of storage since I've been back." Originally, Janice had only planned to stay in California for six months, so she left her motorcycle behind when she moved. She ended up only getting to ride it in the spring and summer on her few trips back east.

"I find that hard to believe. I know how much you love to ride."

Did she ever. Especially riding him.

"I will eventually."

Her first motorcycle had been an entry-level model, a used Harley Sportster 883 Superlow. Since then, she'd bought two more bikes—or hogs, as Harleys were called—the latest being a Harley-Davidson Street Glide in Wicked Red. She'd had to lower the seat height so she could handle the weight of the bike safely, but she loved the power of that machine. Her baby, as she called it.

Her love of motorcycles started in high school, with a boyfriend who rode a Harley. His parents had been proud members of the Harley Owners Group and gifted him one for his sixteenth birthday. Janice tried to convince her parents to buy her one instead of a car, but that was a no-go. She ended up with a used Toyota. To satisfy her need to participate in the lifestyle, she rented motorcycles on the occasional weekend and went riding alone as an escape from the city and the chaos of her personal life in general.

When she was in her late twenties, her father passed and her mother eventually moved to Florida. But she still bore the emotional scars of their dysfunctional relationship. For as long as she could remember, her parents cheated on each other. According to her mother, "He started it."

They spent most of their marriage trying to one-up each other. There was always some blowup or episode that caused strain, and for that reason, she hated drama. She'd had enough in a household where there was no trust. She didn't know why they bothered staying together. Certainly not for her, because long after she moved out, they remained married.

"I bought a bike myself."

"You did? When?" Janice asked, unable to keep the shock out of her voice.

Nathan chuckled. "Don't sound so surprised. Damn. I rode with you before."

"Renting a bike is not the same as buying one. When did you get it?"

"A couple of years ago. I take it out every so often."

A couple of years ago, while she was in California. It was on the tip of her tongue to invite him on a ride, but she held back. They might not be at the point where that type of conversation was appropriate yet.

"Which one?"

"The Harley Road King."

"Black, of course."

"Of course."

"I can't believe you didn't tell me you bought a motorcycle."

His gaze rested on her for a moment. "How would that come up? We don't see each other except at work, and when we do, we mostly talk about work." He returned his attention to the wheel.

True, sadly. They used to talk for hours on the phone, losing track of time in the middle of engaging conversations and funny stories.

Nathan lowered the car to the ground and stood. "All done. Remember what I told you about speeding."

"Yes, I understand. No more than fifty miles per hour, and I have permission to come in late tomorrow morning so I can get a new tire put on."

"Good." He placed the damaged tire and the tools back in her trunk and shut it. Then he walked over to her and extended his hand.

At first, she was confused, but then she realized he was asking for his clothes. "Oh." She handed them over, and he draped the jacket and tie over his arm. They should go their separate ways now, but she didn't want to. Twirling a lock of hair around her finger, she asked, "How much do I owe you?"

"Service was on the house."

His voice was light, but he watched her with a quietness that made her press on a little more boldly.

"I insist. Maybe I can buy you a late dinner if you haven't had another sandwich from downstairs." She wrinkled her nose to indicate what she thought of the café.

Less than thirty minutes ago, she had been tired and ready to go home, but sharing these brief moments with Nathan energized her and made her want to spend more time in his company. Like they used to.

"I didn't get another sandwich, but I need to head home and make sure my brother hasn't burned the place down." He glanced at his watch.

During the period that she had been in California, Nathan

had become the legal guardian of his younger brother Abram, after Abram's parents passed away during a highway accident while on a road trip.

She had called him immediately when she heard the news, and they'd talked as he tried to sort through the grief of losing his father and stepmother, and the shock of becoming the legal guardian of a teenager. The conversation had occurred only months after she moved to California. It had been brief and his tone stiff, but she was glad she'd called to at least express her condolences, despite their strained relationship status.

"How's Abram doing?" She was prolonging the conversation because she longed for bits of details about him and his life, details to which she was no longer privy.

"Pretty good. I was concerned about his ability to bounce back after losing both his parents at such a young age, but he's adjusted remarkably well."

"That's a testament to the good job his big brother is doing."

"I don't know about that, but I do my best."

"Which I'm sure is a wonderful job."

There had probably been other family members who could have taken in Abram, an aunt or uncle that he knew better. But Nathan had a naturally giving and helpful nature, and though he'd barely known his brother because of the age difference, she wasn't surprised he'd taken him in. His helpfulness at times had posed a problem in their relationship.

One of his exes, whom he called a friend, had packages delivered to his house after she sold her home and was getting ready to move to another state. She even had him watch her cat one week when she went on vacation, but the last straw was when she called late one night, and Nathan went to pick her up when her car broke down on the highway.

Didn't she have anybody else she could call? He didn't see it as a big deal, but their relationship drove Janice crazy. She didn't remain friends with exes the way Nathan did, and if it weren't for the fact that they worked together, she wouldn't have maintained any type of contact with him.

"We'll see. As I said, he's doing well, but he does have his moments. I keep wondering if I was that hyper and such a smart-aleck-know-it-all when I was a kid."

"I can absolutely see you behaving like a know-it-all, Mr. Perfectionist."

"You're a fine one to talk."

"Don't even try it. I'm nothing like you."

"Oh right, you prefer to get drunk and party."

"Nothing wrong with partying from time to time. It's good to let loose. You had fun the times we went clubbing, right?"

He chuckled. Man, he had the best laugh. "Actually, I did."

"See? Thanks to me, you were able to let out your inner wild child," Janice said with a smug lift of one shoulder.

The gaze slowly died on his face, and he glanced at his watch again. "Yeah. Look, I better get out of here. I'll see you tomorrow."

"Are you sure I can't pay you back in some way?"

His face suddenly transformed into hard lines, making his prominent cheekbones even more pronounced. "What do you want, Janice?" he asked in exasperation.

She blinked in shock. "I don't know what you mean."

"You know exactly what I mean. Cut the shit."

Her heart crumbled under the weight of his angry tone. "I was trying to be nice. Cut what shit?"

"Stop screwing with me," Nathan said harshly.

Janice took a step back. "That's not what I'm doing."

"That's what it feels like. You could have easily called road-side assistance to help you, but you asked me. I helped, and we're good. You don't owe me anything."

She swallowed. "All right. But for the record, I chose not to call roadside assistance because I thought they would take too long."

Nathan swore and ran a hand down the back of his head. He turned away from her briefly. When he turned back, the anger was gone and replaced with bleakness in his eyes. "It's better if we keep our relationship the way it's been. We're coworkers. Boss, subordinate. Anything else blurs the lines and creates a situation that could get...complicated, to say the least. And we both know how you hate complicated."

The last statement was an unnecessary jab, and Janice squared her shoulders. "And we both know how you enjoy making sure everybody is happy and being Mr. Helpful, including the women you're no longer screwing."

Nathan chuckled bitterly. "You don't see the irony in that, do you?"

Heat flamed her cheeks. He'd done for her exactly what she'd accused him of doing for other women.

"Let's be perfectly clear. My helpfulness is only part of the problem you had with us."

"There was nothing else. Forgive me if I don't think you should be helping an ex move or keeping her cat while she jaunts off to Europe."

"A couple of times, she fed me home-cooked meals, among other small favors. The relationship was reciprocal, Janice. That's what friendship is. I helped her, she helped me."

"And you don't see that as a problem? This tit-for-tat that you had going on with that woman was a red flag in my book. How else did she help you, Nathan? What other *favors* did she do?"

He shook his head. "This is the kind of bullshit I don't need because you're implying there was more to a purely platonic relationship. Do me a favor and keep your hang-ups to yourself. You may not be able to have platonic relationships with your exes, but some of us can."

The conversation had taken an unexpected turn that Janice no longer enjoyed. "Thank you for your help," she said stiffly.

"You're welcome," Nathan said curtly.

He didn't move, so she walked around to the driver's side of her car. He wouldn't walk away, not until she was safely inside, no matter how annoyed he had become by their conversation.

Janice climbed into the car and mounted her cell phone on the dashboard. Then she watched in the rearview mirror as Nathan's long strides took him quickly to the Mercedes SUV.

She started the Avalon and pulled out of the parking space, and he followed behind her as she wound her way toward the exit of the parking deck. When she pulled into the street, she blinked away the tears that stung her eyes. She didn't know why she was being so emotional. There was simply no reason for her to be all choked up and teary-eyed. So what if her expectations had been dashed? She and Nathan would remain firmly in the same space they'd occupied for the past nine months.

Her fingers tightened on the steering wheel, and she forced her foot hard on the accelerator in an effort to escape her thoughts and feelings.

Her phone chimed, and she glanced at the message from Nathan.

SLOW DOWN.

All caps, as if he were yelling at her, which he'd probably do if he were seated beside her.

Despite her emotional state, she smiled a little, appreciating the reminder. A quick glance in the rearview mirror showed him taking a left, and she continued on her way home, slower, and with a heavy heart.

5

Janice pulled up in the driveway of her best friend Jada Wilson's house, a steel-blue newly renovated bungalow-style home Jada had inherited from her grandfather. The four-bedroom, four-bath house was located in the historic Grant Park neighborhood, two blocks from the park and convenient to the Atlanta BeltLine, a multi-use trail currently under development.

Upon her return to Atlanta nine months ago, Janice had moved in with Jada and their other best friend Soul Carrington while she searched for a house to buy. Accustomed to living by herself for years, Janice hadn't been sure if their roommate situation could work, but after only a few days of settling in, their living arrangement reminded her of their days at Spelman when they were suite mates. Now, she welcomed the opportunity to unwind with her girlfriends, though she'd been here much longer than expected because of the renovation delays.

She climbed the front steps onto the porch where two rocking chairs sat. Inside, her heels clicked on the oak floor as she bypassed the other rooms and walked straight toward the light coming from the open kitchen in the back.

The house's modern design aesthetic was a testament to Jada's great eye. As an interior designer who'd recently started her own design firm, she'd chosen to keep most of the walls white while adding contemporary, stylish furniture throughout in a minimalist design. The result was an airy space under soaring ceilings that was practically a showpiece. It was nice to come home to such an uncluttered, lovely home each day.

Janice walked into the kitchen with its white cabinets and found Jada standing at the short bar that separated the kitchen from the breakfast nook, with a bowl of ice cream beside her. Her curvy friend had chocolate-brown skin and almond-shaped eyes. Head bent over her sketchpad with strands of her shoulder-length hair tucked behind an ear, she worked on a design with a charcoal pencil. Ever since she'd known Jada, she was always sketching out ideas on a pad.

"Hey," Janice said, joining her friend at the counter.

Jada looked up in surprise. She'd been so engrossed in her work, she obviously hadn't heard Janice enter. "Hey." She frowned. "You okay?"

Janice shrugged. "I've been better." Her feelings were still bruised from the conversation with Nathan.

Jada straightened. "You look like you could use some of this." She slid over the carton of vanilla chocolate chip ice cream and handed over a spoon that she pulled from the utensils drawer. She then took a bowl from the cabinet and set it in front of Janice.

"You know me so well." Gratefully, Janice dipped her spoon into the carton and scooped ice cream into a bowl. When she was finished, she placed the container in the freezer.

"What's on your mind?"

Janice shrugged. "Everything and nothing. Work, the progress on my house. Nathan Crenshaw."

Jada's eyebrows raised higher. "That's a name I haven't heard in a while. Did something happen at work?"

"After work. He helped me change a tire in the parking deck tonight. During the course of our conversation, he said something that threw me. He told me to stop screwing with him."

"What the heck does that mean?"

She explained the circumstances around the conversation, and when she was finished, her friend frowned thoughtfully.

"Sounds like he still has feelings for you."

"Which would be crazy, right? I don't know what to think. But if he does still have feelings for me, maybe that wouldn't be so bad." She spoke in a softer voice toward the end.

"Oh, really? Are you saying you still have feelings for him?"

Jada's surprise was not unwarranted. Despite the closeness with her friends, she'd never actually divulged to them that she still carried a torch for her ex. As far as they knew, when she broke up with him and left for California, that was the end of their relationship, and she'd moved on. She went through a period of mourning, but because the relationship was so short-lived, they didn't know that her feelings for him went deeper than the surface. Of course, seeing her dive into the dating scene right away cemented that idea, as well as seeing her date multiple men since her return to Atlanta.

"Most times I think our breakup was a good decision, but here I am almost three years later, wondering..."

Wondering and searching for the level of excitement with other men that she'd experienced with him. Searching for the sense of comfort that came with the security of a man like Nathan.

"Maybe...I don't know, maybe we should try again. I just have to show him that I'm worth the risk." Janice spooned ice cream into her mouth.

"Wow. If anyone else were telling me this, I'd say it was completely normal to have feelings for an ex, especially if you still worked together. Coming from you, the idea of you and Nathan getting back together sounds crazy. You cut off your exes as soon as the relationship is over, and you never double-dip in a relationship."

"Maybe I should rethink my stance. Maybe I'll make an exception for Nathan." Janice glanced away from the sheer confusion in Jada's eyes and scooped up the bowl. "I better go to bed. Nathan put the donut on my car, and I'm going in early to the mechanic shop to get a new tire. And who knows, maybe I'll have an epiphany when I wake up and know exactly what I need to do."

"I'll keep my fingers crossed for you," Jada said.

"Thanks. By the way, where's Soul?"

"She's staying late at the studio tonight to work with one of her students." Soul used to tour with a dance troupe, but after one too many injuries, she retired and opened a dance studio. Now she taught instead.

"All right. I'll catch up with her tomorrow. Good night."

Janice climbed the stairs to her bedroom. Although she'd told Jada she might wake up with an epiphany, she already knew what she'd do, she just didn't know how yet.

Somehow, someway, she had to get Nathan back.

THE CONDOMINIUM WAS quiet when Nathan entered. Quiet and dark.

The two-bedroom unit opened to a sunken living room and a bank of windows that looked out onto the Atlanta nightscape, and it was filled with heavy dark brown leather furniture surrounding a massive mahogany table. He hadn't owned the place very long. He bought it after he became his brother's legal guardian. Before that, he lived in a one-bedroom apartment that had been sufficient for his bachelor lifestyle.

Walking slowly, he skirted the living room and headed toward the bedrooms. Abram's bedroom door was ajar, so he eased the door open and peeked in on his brother. The desk lamp was still on, and Abram had his eyes closed, but he was fake sleeping. He'd probably hopped in bed as soon as he heard Nathan open the front door.

At least he hasn't burned the place down, Nathan thought with a wry smile.

Most nights, he came home at a reasonable hour, and it helped that he could work remotely if he needed to finish up a project. But sometimes working late couldn't be helped, especially with the volunteer project recently assigned by the president. There would probably be a few more late nights like this, but not too many, he hoped.

At least Abram was sixteen and old enough to fend for himself. If he needed anything urgently, he knew to call Nathan or contact the building concierge.

Nathan eased the door shut and went a few doors down to his own bedroom. He stripped out of the day's clothes and tossed them in the hamper in his dressing room.

His bedroom was simply furnished, with dark gray textured wallpaper, dark carpet, and a black leather headboard attached to a king-size bed covered in gray and white linens. He set his watch atop the gleaming walnut bookshelf that sat below a window which gave him an unobstructed view of the city. Janice had never seen this room because he bought the condo after they broke up, but he could imagine she'd have plenty to say about the monochromatic decor.

As he slipped on some running shorts, he quietly cursed himself for thinking about her. He had barely spent twenty minutes isolated with her, and now she dominated the thoughts in his head. No surprise there.

He had no problem keeping in touch with his exes if they wanted to remain in touch. A lot of people didn't understand his stance, but he'd seen his father use women all his life, including Nathan's mother, whom he'd never married. The last thing he wanted was to be that kind of man. A user. Someone who hit it and quit it.

Monogamy worked fine for him, and so did maintaining friendships with his exes. It wasn't hard to be cordial when you made an effort to do so. And it kept the breakups from being dramatic explosions, which he'd seen often enough when his father ended his liaisons.

How many weekends had he spent with his father when some woman had come knocking in the middle of the night, cursing and yelling at him to open the door? His father always parked his car in the garage because if he parked in the drive-way, he risked waking up to keyed doors or lewd accusations spray-painted on the side—both of which had happened.

That shit had to be stressful as hell. Nathan didn't need that in his life. Treat people the way you want to be treated, and then you didn't have to worry about those types of situations, and in the end, he added to his friendship circle. Janice had never understood that, and they hadn't maintained a friendship after they broke up, which wasn't entirely her fault.

Working with her had to be one of the hardest things he'd ever had to do because he didn't want to simply work with her. He wanted her.

Had wanted her, he corrected. Past tense.

"That's over and done with," he muttered to himself. But he did have to be careful and keep his distance.

The phone rang, and when he glanced at the number, his brooding immediately stopped when he saw the photo of a woman with light brown skin and a short bob appear on the screen.

"Hey, babe." Nathan made his way out of the room.

He and Sherilyn Tomes had been together for over a year now, and she was nothing like Janice. Sherilyn wore her straight black hair in sleek, simple styles that didn't grab atten-tion. No bright colors. No motorcycles. No red hair.

"When did you get in?" she asked.

"A few minutes ago." Nathan stepped down into the living room and crossed the floor to the kitchen. "I'm about to fix a snack before I go to bed."

"How about some conversation while you do that?"

"I'd love that. How was your day?"

"Better now that I'm talking to you."

He smiled and opened the refrigerator. "Same here."

6

"Hold the elevator!" Precious yelled, rushing toward the closing doors.

Janice hit the Open button, and the doors sprang apart.

Precious hopped in, mildly out of breath. "Thank you! Whew. Either I'm out of shape or old age is getting to me."

Janice laughed before returning her attention to the iPad in her hand. "We're the same age, so I'm hoping it's not so-called old age."

"I hear you." After a brief pause, Precious said, "I have a secret, and you can't tell a soul."

"A secret about what?" Janice studied the notes she'd taken on her iPad. She spent her lunch break going through a backlog of emails from the staff she supervised along the east coast and pinned the ones she wanted her admin to follow up on.

"He's getting married," Precious said in a hushed voice.

"Who's getting married?" Janice murmured, still distracted as she perused a new email that had come in.

"Who do you think? Nathan."

Janice's head popped up. She stared at Precious. "What are you talking about?"

"Brauge Jewelers hand-delivered a package this morning. I was curious, but there was no way for me to know what was going on without outright asking Nathan. I got lucky later when I went into his office. I caught him standing in front of his desk, staring at an open ring box with a frown on his face—as if he was wondering if he'd spent enough money on the ring, or was it good enough. You know, the kind of thing I imagine men contemplate when they purchase an engagement ring. As soon as he saw me, he snapped the box closed and shoved it in his pocket. But I saw it. It's a large stone, marquise cut, brilliant. He's going to be off the market soon." Precious sighed dramatically.

Janice's stomach plunged with dizzying speed.

Brauge Jewelers was a high-end store that specialized in diamond rings and other fine jewelry. If a man wanted to impress a woman, he bought her a ring from Brauge.

"I didn't know he was seeing anyone seriously."

"Oh, he is. She stopped in twice that I know of, but it was months apart. The first time, I made dinner reservations for them. The second time, he came rushing out of his office in a panic because he'd forgotten to order flowers for her birthday. I handled it swiftly, and he was relieved because he was on his way to a meeting with the higher-ups and didn't have time to do it himself. That was about three months ago, but I'm pretty sure they're still seeing each other, and now it looks like he's about to pop the question. I should be happy for him, but I'm *so* jealous of her."

"Who is she?" Janice asked, trying to sound mildly interested though she was *very* interested in learning everything she could about this mystery woman. And why didn't she know anything about her? Not once had Nathan said a word about being seriously involved with anyone.

The elevator opened on their floor, and both women stepped out.

"Her name is Sherilyn Tomes, and she works as an office manager at a private investigation firm, or something like that. That's literally all I know because he rarely mentions her, and except for the two times he involved me, he makes all arrangements for them."

Janice digested the information in silence.

Precious leaned in. "She's tall and very pretty. I don't know what prompted him to pop the question, but it's about time. He's a little older than us, isn't he?"

Janice swallowed as acid built in her stomach. "By a few years. He's thirty-nine," she said absentmindedly. Her head throbbed, and she pressed a hand to her temple.

Nathan was getting engaged. Probably this weekend.

"I'm going to the ladies' room. See you later," Precious called out, hurrying off.

Janice should go to her own office but stood in the middle of the carpeted floor. Feeling lost and confused, she slowly tucked the iPad into her purse.

Nathan was getting engaged.

Her breathing became shallow as her chest heaved up and down.

Nathan was getting engaged?

Her feet marched straight ahead in the direction of his office. She needed answers.

She bypassed Precious's empty office but wouldn't have stopped anyway if she were in there. She knocked once and then shoved her way in and slammed the door behind her.

Nathan looked up from behind the large cherrywood desk, pen poised in one hand, a frown furrowing his brow.

"You're getting married?" She blurted the question without thinking.

The frown deepened. "What did you say?"

She moved closer. "I heard you're getting engaged. Is that true?"

He swore under his breath and tossed the pen onto the desk, a clear indication that what she'd heard was true.

"Were you going to tell me?"

"I was," he said evenly.

"Not that you owe me anything, but—"

"We were lovers, and we work together. Of course, I intended to tell you. I've been so busy with work and this project for Nina Winthrop, I've hardly had time to think about anything else, much less call and tell you what was going on."

Lovers. Over time, he'd used different words to describe their togetherness. They'd gone from being in a relationship to having an affair, to simply being lovers. The downgraded status of their relationship stung.

"You had time to pick out a ring and have it hand-delivered to the office."

He didn't respond at first, seemingly stunned by the information she had. "Listen—"

"How long have you been seeing her?"

"About a year and a half," Nathan answered in a clipped voice.

"That's a long time. When are you going to ask her?" Stomach tense, she waited.

"This weekend, and I was going to tell you *after* the engagement was official. How did you find out about the delivery?" His eyes narrowed. "And why does my engagement matter to you?"

"Because..." She didn't have a good answer, except that the crushing, oppressive pain in her chest had compelled her to act. "It's kind of quick, isn't it? And a bit hypocritical, considering last week you were reminding me about how much I need a real man in my life—presumably you. Your loyalty to this woman—"

Nathan stood up with such force, his chair careened backward and bumped into the window behind him. Pointing a finger at Janice, he leaned over the desk and said, "Don't come in here preaching to me about loyalty. You walked away six months into our relationship and didn't look back. We had something, but it wasn't important to you. So if you came in here to chastise me, save your breath and take a long, hard look in the mirror."

"You have some nerve! The CFO gave me an assignment in California to straighten out that office," Janice said.

"You *volunteered*. You didn't have to go, and you didn't have to stay for two years."

"They needed me!" Janice yelled.

"And I didn't?" he shouted back.

Silence pounded through the room.

Chest heaving with emotion, Janice stared across the desk. "What do you want me to say? You didn't exactly fight for us to stay together. You walked away as soon as I said no."

Nathan's brows snapped together. "What does that mean?"

She pressed her lips together. She'd said too much.

"What does that mean, Janice?" His eyebrows sank deeper over his eyes.

"Nothing. I wish you the best. You're a good man. The best. Adored by many. She's a lucky woman." She meant the words even though she'd purposely said them in a sarcastic tone.

Nathan marched within several feet of her. "I didn't think badgering you would make any difference because your mind was made up. You booked your flight before you told me the news, not once considering me. And let's not forget that you must have told me a hundred times how much you hate drama in relationships because you saw enough of what a bad relationship looked like when you were growing up. Hell, we bonded over that because you know the deal with my father and the way he treated every other woman but Abram's mother. Was I supposed to tie you to a chair and cancel your reservations? Are you saying if I'd fought harder, you would have—"

"Don't read more into what I said. I said what I meant and meant what I said. There are no hidden meanings in my words."

She had booked the flight before talking to him about the trip, but only because she didn't want him to talk her out of it. She had needed to get away from him, and going all the way to California to escape how he made her feel had made sense at the time. In retrospect, she might have tossed away the love of her life because she was scared.

Nathan shook his head. "You know what your problem is? You play too many games, and that's why your ass is single right now."

The words landed like a hard slap to the cheek, shocking her and making her face hot. She shot him her most venomous glare. "I am single because I want to be. And for the record, I don't play games."

"No? Not even a week after I talked to you about you and me and a future together, you volunteered to go to California. The word forever made you panic. You're a runner, Janice. I saw that when we were involved, and I thought I could overcome it. You overthink and overanalyze every damn thing, looking for flaws. And when you don't find any, you assume they're hidden, and you jump ship anyway."

"That is *not* true."

"It *is* true. All that analyzing works great here in the office, pouring over financials and searching for trends in facts and figures, but that's not the way to handle relationships."

"You don't know anything about me and how I handle relationships," Janice in a low tone, voice vibrating with defensive anger.

"I know plenty based on what you've told me about your past boyfriends and your broken engagement. But whatever issues you have, you have to work them out within yourself. And you have to be the one to let people in."

"And why exactly would I let anyone like you in? You talk out of both sides of your mouth, Nathan. One minute you're hitting on me, the next minute I find out you're about to be engaged. *You* are the reason why women like me have trust issues."

"No, we're not doing this. You have trust issues because of your father and your ex. I'm nothing like either one of them. You choose not to see what's right in front of your face. What you don't appreciate, someone else will."

The words struck close to home because she'd had the very same thought. Had she lost out on a perfectly good man because of her fears?

The man she'd been engaged to—the one who'd bailed on her days before their wedding—had paled in comparison to Nathan. The heightened emotions and lack of control she experienced with Nathan had scared her. He had consumed her. She had wanted to spend every minute with him, tell him everything, and be absorbed into his world.

Maybe she had run scared, and now she'd lost any hope of being with him again. Well, she would not give him the satisfaction of knowing about her regrets.

"You know what, one of us is a little too full of himself. On second thought, I wish this poor woman luck because apparently, all the women that you work with have given you a big head." Janice swung around and walked away from him.

"Keep pretending you don't care, Janice. I hope pretending keeps you warm at night."

Gritting her teeth, she swung back around. His arms were folded across his chest, his lush lips set in a firm line.

Her breasts ached for the familiar tug of those lips, which would be off-limits soon. Knowing she could never touch him or have him touch her again fueled her ire.

"Maybe you should look more deeply into your own thought processes. I saw the way you ogled my legs the other day. Are you sure you're marrying this woman because you want to, or because you can't have me?"

A flash of anger sparked in his dark eyes.

With a satisfied harrumph, Janice exited his office and slammed the door again.

7

"How much is that going to cost me?" Janice asked.

A lousy week had gone from bad to worse. On Tuesday she found out Nathan was seeing someone seriously and getting engaged this weekend. Yesterday, Precious cornered her in the break room and tearfully demanded how she could betray her trust and tell Nathan what she knew. Though she promised the admin she hadn't said a word to Nathan about where she learned about his engagement and pledged to smooth over the situation, Precious begged her not to. She didn't want any more trouble, and Janice understood.

Now there were more problems with the house she was renovating. She sat in the car outside the home she shared with her friends, talking to the contractor in charge of the work, which had taken a lot longer than she'd anticipated and was expected to go well over budget.

Seconds ago, the head of Reynolds Construction, Theodore Reynolds—an older man who claimed he'd been in the business for over forty years—told her about another issue. It seemed there was always some delay or problem cropping up.

Last month was asbestos contamination. Now she had to deal with faulty wiring.

Initially, Reynolds said the renovations would take six months, tops. She'd hoped to have moved into the house by now, but there was much more wrong than they knew—or so he claimed—and the timeline was continuously pushed back. She didn't know how much more bad news she could take.

"At least a couple thousand dollars more I'd figure, but I won't know until I get the full estimate," Theodore said in his gravelly voice. "I'll get a couple of quotes like I did before and have those for you by the end of next week. Don't worry, we'll get everything done. I promise."

"Doesn't feel like it," Janice grumbled.

He laughed. "This isn't unusual, especially with a house that age. Don't worry your sweet little head about anything, we'll have you good to go in no time."

Janice frowned, wondering for the umpteenth time if he were being honest or scamming her. Granted, when she found the place, the house had gone into foreclosure, had boarded-up windows, and a multitude of other issues. But she'd fallen in love with its potential and bought it with cash, then hired Reynolds Construction to do the necessary renovations.

"I'll wait to hear from you with those estimates by the end of next week."

They said goodbye, and she sat in the car, contemplating what to do next. Theodore Reynolds had come highly recommended by the real estate agent, so she was hesitant to get another contractor. Would they be better or take advantage?

She exited the vehicle and flung her bag over her shoulder. Tonight, she looked forward to shedding the burden of her thoughts with the two women she loved and trusted as much as sisters. She and her girlfriends were all busy with work, dating, and life, but they still scheduled a monthly girls' night which they took turns planning. Because she didn't cook, she'd purchased dinner.

She picked up the food from the back seat—a small pan of lasagna, salad, breadsticks, and wine. Balancing the containers, she walked up the driveway and took the stairs up onto the front porch.

"Honeys, I'm home!" she called as she entered.

"We're back here!" That was Soul.

Janice found both of her friends in the kitchen.

Jada sat at the bar, and Soul stood on the opposite side, facing her. With smooth dark skin and a lithe body poured into skinny jeans and a tank top, she looked every bit the dancer that she was. Glasses of wine sat on the stone counter in front of them.

"You started without me," Janice said, looking pointedly at the glasses.

"You're late," Soul said.

"They messed up the order, *and* I had a wonderful conversation with the contractor on my way here." Janice heaved out a heavy breath.

Jada groaned. "More problems?"

"Yes." Janice set the food on the countertop. "Let me go change, and I'll be right back."

She hurried upstairs to her room and swiftly changed into a pair of baggy purple shorts and an oversized yellow T-shirt that draped off one shoulder. Padding into the kitchen on bare feet, she saw that Jada had placed an enormous portion of lasagna on a plate and was putting part of it in her mouth.

Janice raised her eyebrows at the sight and turned to Soul. "What's wrong with her? She only eats like that when she's sad."

"Nothing's wrong with me," Jada said around a mouthful of pasta and meat. She swallowed. "Sorry, I'm starving. I skipped lunch. Big mistake."

"Actually, she's in a great mood," Soul said slyly. "Solomon sent her flowers today out of the blue."

Janice did a little wiggle, followed by jazz hands. "Oooo. What for?"

"To let her know he's happy for her that she's starting her design business."

"Well, well, well. Isn't that sweet."

Jada rolled her eyes. "You know we're only friends."

Soul laughed. "Yeah, whatever. Let's move into the living room so Janice can tell us what else is going on with the house."

Minutes later, they all settled in the living room. Jada sat cross-legged on the floor with her wine and plate on the coffee table. Janice sat on the sofa with her plate on her legs, and Soul did the same on the other end of the sofa.

"What's the latest on the renovations?" Jada asked.

Janice felt almost guilty telling them about the problems because Jada had recommended a different contractor. She updated them, explaining about the wiring problem that was causing another delay.

"Are you sure this guy is telling the truth?" Soul asked.

"I hope so, or I'm wasting a lot of time and money. He said I'll have the new estimate by next week."

Going over budget was anathema to her finance brain, particularly since she'd already included an overrun cushion into the calculations. But what could she do? She didn't have much knowledge about renovating a house, which was why she'd asked for recommendations. Compared to the other contractors, Reynolds Construction had given her a mid-range quote and seemed trustworthy at the time. Now she wasn't so sure.

Soul shook her head. "Sheesh, it's like you bought the house in *The Money Pit*. Remember that movie?"

"I know. I'm starting to get depressed. Jada, I hope you don't mind that I'll have to stay here longer. I feel so bad about this."

"You know good and well that doesn't matter to me. I told you that you could stay as long as you need to, and I meant it. Do you need the name of the contractor I recommended to you when you started this project? The one you didn't choose?" Jada flashed a grin.

Janice winced, wondering if she'd made a mistake not listening to her friend. "No, I still have his information. Tomas Molina, right?"

"Right. He costs more, but he's worth it."

"Okay. I'll make my decision about what to do in a few days."

"What else is going on with you?" Soul picked at the food on her plate, which was mostly salad with only a smidge of lasagna. She never ate much.

"Last night I couldn't sleep." Janice shrugged.

"Would your lack of sleep have anything to do with Nathan's plans this weekend?"

She had told them in an offhand manner about his pending engagement, pretending that it didn't matter much to her. In truth, she couldn't get it out of her mind.

"Of course not."

Soul arched an eyebrow. "Come on, it's us. You can be honest, finally."

"I'm always honest with you guys." Janice's eyes bounced between her two friends, somewhat surprised by the skepticism etched into their faces.

"You don't feel anything at all that he's getting married to someone else? No jealousy and none of the old feelings have resurfaced?"

Janice shrugged again, but the weight in her chest belied her true feelings. She opened her mouth to save face, but couldn't go through with the lie. Her shoulders sagged, and she cradled her wine glass, staring down into the depths of the burgundy liquid.

"Sweetie, be honest," Jada said gently. "It's okay to admit you're affected by his engagement."

"He deserves to be happy. I'm happy for him," Janice said dully.

"You don't *sound* happy," Soul said carefully.

Janice swallowed. "I am. I'm happy for him. She's probably perfect, and they'll have a perfect life together."

"That could have been you," Soul said.

The words rubbed salt in her wounded heart. "We're incompatible."

"You made a great couple," Soul countered.

"I agree." Jada sipped her wine.

"I would agree with you both, except you know what happened the last time I thought I was part of a great couple. My fiancé broke off our engagement and ran off with his stepmother."

"I always knew their relationship seemed fishy," Jada muttered bitterly.

Janice couldn't argue. Once or twice she'd wondered if something was going on between her fiancé and his stepmother but quickly set aside such a ludicrous thought. She couldn't fathom how anyone could sleep with his own father's wife. She'd literally been in the middle of a tawdry soap opera and missed the red flags. Never again.

"I like my life right now. I'm working on the renovations —granted, those could be better—and my career is great. I don't need a man in the mix to mess things up. Certainly not a man that I work with and used to have a relationship with."

"So you made a mistake once. That doesn't mean Nathan will also cause you heartache. I think he's great," Soul said.

"He is great. Great for someone else," Janice said firmly. "Besides, if I were even remotely interested in getting involved with him, that ship has sailed. By the end of this weekend, he'll be officially engaged and marrying someone else." Janice gulped her wine.

"I would pick you for him," Jada said.

"I would pick you for him, too," Soul said.

Janice smiled faintly. "I get it. You think that we'd be a great couple, but the truth is, we didn't work out."

"And why was that?" Soul said.

"Don't start," Janice warned.

"Soul has a point," Jada spoke up.

"You too, Jada?"

Jada shrugged. "You have a habit of...how do I put this delicately... breaking up with men before they have a chance to break up with you."

"I do not!"

Soul stared at her. "Yes, you do."

Nathan had said something similar, except he'd called her a runner. She might be able to deny the accusation from him, but she couldn't from her girls. They knew her too well.

Ever since her broken engagement six years ago, she treated men like worn socks that needed to be changed every six to eight months. Was that why she'd jumped at the chance to go to California around the six-month mark in her relationship with Nathan? The evidence didn't lie.

Blinking back tears, she hoarsely admitted, "I was crying in the wine store."

"Oh, honey, I'm sorry. Here, have some more wine." Soul leaned forward and emptied the bottle into Janice's glass.

Grateful, Janice cradled the glass in her hand. "Change of subject."

They had an agreement, that when one person announced *Change of subject*, they had to change the subject. It meant the conversation had gone too far.

"Weather's been nice lately," Soul said right away.

"Sure has. I'm thinking about having the yard guy plant

some flowers along the front of the house. What do you guys think?" Jada asked.

Lost in melancholy thoughts, Janice let them go back and forth without contributing to the conversation.

"You know what we haven't done in a long time?" Soul suddenly asked.

"What?" Jada asked plopping the last of a breadstick into her mouth.

"Dance it out." Soul turned her head slowly in Janice's direction.

"*No,*" Janice wailed.

Dance it out had become a regular routine back at Spelman College. Soul came home frustrated one night from one of her dance performance classes, and Janice had been distraught over a math exam that kicked her butt. It had been her idea to dance away their worry. Soul took the lead, choreographing the steps, and they performed a full three-minute routine in the common area of their suite.

When Jada showed up, she joined in, and that became their thing for a while—to dance it out whenever they were worried, angry, or hurting. The last time they danced it out was after Janice's broken engagement.

"You're the one who started it, so it's your fault." Soul set aside her food and Janice's. Then she grabbed Janice by the wrist and hauled her to her feet.

"Song?" Jada picked up her phone and started scrolling through options.

"'Beat It,' Michael Jackson." Before the song came on, Soul started gracefully moving to the beat in her head.

Jada selected the song and music came bursting through the wireless speakers. She squealed and joined Soul.

"Come on, Janice, you know you want to." Soul grabbed her by the hand and forced her into a smooth spin.

"You two get on my nerves!" Janice yelled, but her head started bouncing, and soon, her body was, too.

She danced around the living room with her best friends. Hips swaying, hands in the air, singing "Beat it!" at the top of her lungs.

And for a few minutes, she forgot all about the heaviness in her heart.

8

N athan tightened the tie around his neck and gazed at his reflection in the floor-length mirror in the dressing room of his condo. Tonight he'd decided to wear more color and wore dress slacks with an aquamarine button-down and a paisley tie with the same blue hue prominent in the design.

He walked into the bedroom and spread his arms wide. "How do I look?"

Sixteen-year-old Abram sat on the end of the bed. His skin was a lighter shade of brown than Nathan's, and in Nathan's opinion, he looked more like his mother than their father, with his round face and long lashes above dark eyes. He was born after his father married a much younger woman. A woman Nathan's mother referred to as a product of his father's midlife crisis.

His father had been a terrible partner to his mother—regularly cheating on her and in general, not taking their relationship seriously. Yet by all accounts, he'd been a great husband to Abram's mother and a better father to Abram before he passed.

Perhaps he'd seen them as a second chance, to make up for past mistakes.

Abram brother tilted his head to the side. "Um, you should lose the tie," he said definitively.

"You sure?"

"Yes."

Nathan removed it, opened the top button, and stood still for his brother's inspection.

"Better."

"You're not just saying that?"

"Come on, man, when have I ever not told you the truth?" Nathan opened his mouth to answer, but Abram quickly interrupted him. "Never mind! But I'm telling the truth now."

When Abram first came to live with him after his parents passed away, they experienced growing pains for a few months when he rebelled against Nathan's authority. Because of the age difference, they hadn't been close, and to have Nathan become his guardian, supervisor, and rule enforcer had been problematic for Abram.

After some time, they learned to function, with an interesting mix of a brother–father dynamic. The lying had also declined dramatically, but not completely. Abram was, after all, a sixteen-year-old. But he was much more respectful, his grades had improved, and Nathan didn't have to worry about him acting out or breaking the rules to purposely piss him off.

"I'm ready. She's never seen me in this shirt. Besides, she's not going to say no because of the shirt I'm wearing."

Abram nodded vigorously. "True dat."

Nathan walked over to the bookshelf by the window and picked up the black velvet box. The marquise diamond glinted up at him. At one time, before Janice ran off to California, he had considered giving her a ring.

Shaking his head, he snapped the box shut. No point in

dwelling on the past. She made her decision, and he made his. They'd both moved on.

"Let me see it again." Abram held out his hand.

Nathan handed over the box, and Abram examined the jewelry.

"This is nice, man. Sherilyn is going to definitely say yes."

"Women don't say yes because of the ring. They say yes because they love you."

"I'm pretty sure the ring helps," Abram said.

"If a woman only wants you for a ring, you have a problem."

"Sure. Whatever. When are you going to pop the question during dinner?"

"After dessert. I'm wondering if I even want to do it in front of everyone, or step out onto the balcony of the restaurant to ask her in private."

"You should step out onto the balcony and ask her in private," Abram said with a firm nod.

"Why do you say that?" Nathan asked, amused.

"In case she says no. Then you won't be embarrassed in front of all those people."

Nathan snatched back the ring. "She's not going to say no. Thanks for the vote of confidence."

Abram laughed. "There's a fifty-fifty chance that she'll say no. You might as well make it as least embarrassing for you as possible, in case she does."

"Again, thanks for the vote of confidence," Nathan said dryly.

"I'm looking out for you, the way you look out for me."

Nathan headed out the door, with Abram following behind him. He stepped down into the sunken living room. "You're sure you'll be fine by yourself overnight?" After asking Sherilyn to marry him, he intended to stay at her place.

Abram let out an exaggerated weary groan. "Don't worry

about me. I have popcorn, I'll probably order pizza for dinner, and there are plenty of shows on cable for me to watch."

"Okay. I replenished the cash in the jar in the kitchen, in case you need any."

"I got this. I'm sixteen, not six."

"But it's the first time I'm leaving you alone overnight. I don't know...I'm a little worried." He frowned.

"Nothing's going to happen. Go ahead and pop the question so I can get my new stepmom." He did air quotes. "If for some crazy reason a problem crops up, I promise to call."

"All right. Wish me luck."

"You don't need it, but good luck. I mean, she would be a fool not to say yes. Where is she going to find a better man than you?"

Nathan turned back around, and Abram's cheeks turned a little red. He was clearly embarrassed about the compliment, which in his case was considered effusive.

"Thank you."

Abram shrugged. "Whatever, man."

He took off toward the kitchen, and Nathan smiled as he exited toward his destiny.

And he ignored the niggling doubt at the back of his head that suggested he might be asking the wrong woman for her hand in marriage.

NOTTE WAS one of the best Italian restaurants in town. Though large, it had an intimate ambiance thanks to the dark wood walls, dimmed lights, and votive candles flickering on each table.

As Sherilyn placed the last of the cheesecake into her mouth, Nathan smiled across the table at her. Earlier in the evening, he'd proudly stepped into the crowded restaurant with her on his arm.

She looked fantastic in a long black skirt and fitted blouse that showed off her figure. She was almost as tall as he was in heels, athletic, and in general good company, though she had a few negatives. She could be a little dramatic at times and took her job as an office manager for an investigator a little too seriously, as if she actually worked the cases instead of only paid the bills and answered the phones. But she had other qualities he appreciated. She loved to cook and enjoyed sporting events as much as he did.

Sherilyn dabbed the corners of her mouth with the napkin. "Excuse me while I go to the restroom. When the waiter swings back around, would you let him know that I'd like to have my coffee topped off?"

"Absolutely. You go ahead, and I'll get him over here for a refill for both of us."

She blew him a kiss.

Nathan stood as she left the table and then reclaimed his seat when she walked away. He waved over the waiter and had their coffees topped off. Sipping the dark brew, he briefly touched the bulge of the ring box in his right pocket.

He shouldn't be thinking about her, but his mind strayed to Janice and their confrontation. *Are you sure you're marrying this woman because you want to, or because you can't have me?*

He swore quietly.

Why was he thinking about her right now? Why was he thinking about the vibrant red hair that framed her face or how he had never been able to forget the sensation of her mouth against his?

Janice was a great kisser. Her mouth was a haven of goodness, whether she was on her knees or showering affection on his lips. Her kisses were as high-inducing as cocaine and could drain him of all coherent thought, leaving nothing but the need to claim and own and possess. Damn, he wished he could forget everything about her, but that proved impossible since they worked together.

He ran a hand down his face. He could forget. Their relationship was in the past, and he had a bright future with Sherilyn.

She returned to the table, and he politely stood as she sat down before he reclaimed his chair again.

Face beaming, she reached across the table. "Dinner was great. Thank you for bringing me here. You take such good care of me."

Nathan took her hand. "I'm glad you feel that way. Let's go out onto the balcony and get some fresh air."

"Okay."

He took her by the hand as they stepped away from the table, cutting a path to the back of the restaurant. They went through the French doors and stepped out into the cool night air. There were no tables out here. It was reserved for smokers or anyone who wanted to snuggle after the heavy food they ate.

"This is nice." Sherilyn lifted her face to the dark sky.

Nathan decided to speak entirely off-the-cuff, ridding himself of the rehearsed speech he had practiced. "Sherilyn, I brought you out here for a reason. To tell you that I want to continue taking care of you—for us to take care of each other."

He lowered onto one knee. She gasped, eyes widening as he reached into his pocket and pulled out the box. He flipped open the lid to expose the brilliant diamond ring inside.

"Sherilyn, would you do me the honor of becoming my wife?"

9

Janice tossed her pen on the desk and removed her gold-framed glasses. Flopping her head against the back of the leather chair in her office, she let out a heavy sigh.

She should go home. This had been a long and trying week, and she wasn't going to get any more work done now than she did spending most of the day thinking about the fact that Nathan was now an engaged man.

At least she'd finally taken a ride on the Harley. Last Saturday morning she'd had her mechanic get her bike ready. He'd done the usual maintenance, like bleed the brake fluid, and after checking the steering-head for looseness, tightened it fully.

She went on an hour-long ride on Highway 20, coasting in between cars and letting the sound of the wind and the powerful motor drown out the numbing pain. By the time she returned home, her mind was clear and the knot in her stomach, while it hadn't disappeared completely, had lessened.

Janice stood and stretched her hands above her head. A trip

to the bathroom, and then she'd gather up her belongings and head out.

On the way back from the bathroom, her footsteps slowed when she heard a noise down the hall in the direction of Nathan's office. She'd assumed she was the only one left on the floor. Curious, she peeked down the hall and saw him walking away, eyes trained on a sheaf of papers in his hands.

Right away, her insides crumbled in silent agony. Off the market, and she hadn't made a single move to stop it. If anything, she'd pushed him further away.

With sudden resolve, Janice was determined to be a grown-up and help Nathan celebrate his pending nuptials. She went back to her office and picked up a bottle of rum and a can of Coke from her mini-bar. Rum and Coke was his favorite drink, so what better way to celebrate?

Nathan's door was ajar when she walked up. She peered in and saw him seated on the black sofa with his head thrown back, eyes closed, and arms stretched across the back.

She knocked on the doorframe, and his head lifted, a frown settling between his brows when he saw her. She waited uncertainly for the invitation to enter. He looked...worn. As if he'd had a rough day.

"Should I come back?"

"No. Come in."

She entered and quietly closed the door behind her. She cleared her throat. "First of all, I want to apologize for my behavior the other day when I found out about your upcoming engagement. Of course, you don't owe me anything—not an explanation or..." He wore a blank expression on his face. "Is there something wrong?"

"The weekend didn't go as planned."

"What do you mean?"

He ran a hand down the back of his head. "Sherilyn, the woman I proposed to, turned me down."

"What!" Janice hadn't expected that declaration and quickly crushed the surge of happiness and fixed an empathetic expression on her face. She'd done her best to avoid him all week, certain he was now an engaged man. But he wasn't. "I came in here to help you celebrate, but I assume you can still use these—although for a different reason?" She held up the can and bottle.

"You're right, I can."

"Don't move."

She went over to his mini-bar and mixed the drink the way he liked—plenty of rum and one cube of ice. Then she returned to the sofa and handed over the glass.

Their fingers grazed each other and shivers rippled over her skin. His eyes snapped to hers as if he'd experienced the same sensation.

"Thanks," he murmured.

Janice nodded. She made herself the same drink and then sat on the far end of the sofa. They drank in silence for a minute.

Finally, she asked, "What happened?"

A bitter smile crossed his lips. "You care?"

"Yes, despite what you think." If she ever ran into this Sherilyn woman, she'd kick her butt for hurting him.

Nathan drained the glass and then went over to the mini-bar. Janice kept an eye on his broad back and the way the charcoal-colored slacks hugged his firm behind.

He spoke with his back to her as he fixed another rum and Coke. "She said no. Where have I heard that before?"

Janice grimaced. She'd told him no when he asked her to stay. She told him no when he asked for a long-distance relationship. "Did she give you a reason?"

Nathan walked back to the sofa and sat down. He took a sip before speaking again. "Maybe I should become one of those men who mistreat women."

Clearly, he didn't want to share the reason she'd given him. "You're not that kind of man."

"Never said I was." He took another sip.

"So you're going to turn into an asshole? I can't see it."

"It's certainly an option. Worked for my father. Worked for your father."

"Acting like a jerk won't work for you."

"You sure about that?"

"Yes," Janice said in a hard tone.

He let out a dry, mirthless laugh. Something about his behavior put her on edge. He wasn't himself. He seemed detached, emotionless.

"When you came into my office to confront me about my engagement, you accused me of not telling you about Sherilyn."

"It wasn't an accusation. I simply meant—"

"Do you have a man, Janice?" he asked casually.

The question caught her off guard, so a few seconds elapsed before she answered. "No."

"Not the young guy I saw you with at the movies?"

"No."

"Not dating anyone seriously or casually?"

"No." Where was this conversation going? She shifted.

"You ever try speed dating?"

"I have. I didn't meet anyone I connected with."

"I tried it, too. It didn't work out." He swirled his drink, looking down into the glass with a thoughtful expression.

"I can't believe you went speed dating. You can literally have any woman in this building."

"Can I?" The question hung in the air as heavy and conspicuous as a soaking wet blanket.

The heat of want thumped like a drumbeat between her legs.

His gaze traveled down her body, taking in the fuchsia

ruffled blouse that made her breasts appear bigger, and her long hip-hugging skirt. His nostrils flared ever so slightly.

"Thank you for the drink, but you shouldn't stay here alone with me any longer." Nathan drained the glass and stood abruptly. This time he poured himself a Scotch.

Janice placed her half-finished beverage on the table beside the sofa and stood on unsteady feet. "Why can't I stay?" she asked softly.

"Because I'm horny," he said harshly. "Because I'm feeling a little reckless and that could be bad for you. Because you came in here to help me celebrate a non-existent engagement, and all I can think about is how I'd do anything for a taste of you. A kiss on the cheek. The opportunity to slide my tongue along your collarbone. I want to lick every damn inch of your skin and hold you tight and never let you go because nothing—*no one*—compares to you. And you know what makes this harder to bear? Knowing that you want me to. It's ridiculous that we're not together. You know that, don't you?"

Her tongue swept across her lips, moistening her mouth. "I know," she said in a barely audible voice.

Nathan slammed the glass on the corner of the desk and approached her with firm intention in his gaze. "So why keep fighting it? Give me a good reason why we shouldn't be together. We're both single, and you can't use distance as an excuse anymore. One. Good. Reason."

Janice shook her head. "I don't have one. And I don't want to fight what I feel anymore."

His gaze traced her mouth, and her breath hitched. His eyes darkened, and then his mouth was on top of hers. He kissed her with determination and demand, his all-consuming mouth plucking at her lips, moving in a heavenly caress that required she give him her all.

The first thing she tasted was rich Scotch and then the familiar sweetness of his delicious kisses. Janice heard her own sigh of pleasure as one of his hands fisted in the delicate silk of her blouse as if he were two seconds from tearing the fabric to shreds. Her arms circled around to his back, and their bodies pressed closer together. Like this, she felt every inch of his hard frame against her sensitive nipples, her stomach, and her thighs. There was no escaping his masculine scent or the pressure of his hard male body against hers.

Angling her head to the side, she parted her lips to take his tongue. Their tongues tangled together, sliding and gliding, advancing and retreating in decadent eroticism.

Janice moaned, pressing harder against him and encountered the swollen manifestation of his manhood. She rolled her hips in a forceful grind against his hardness, and then it was Nathan's turn to moan.

This was what she'd wanted. This was what she'd been hiding from. She needed to be touched, caressed, kissed until she was lost in him and drowning in fiery need.

Her head spun in a crazy, dizzying pattern, and still, he didn't stop kissing her, as if he never would. He anchored one hand in her hair and used the other to cup a breast. He kneaded the supple flesh, rubbing his wide thumb over the nipple with lazy indulgence. He had to know he was driving her mad.

He finally released her lips to trail kisses down her chin to her throat. Nuzzling her neck, he whispered, "I've been wanting to kiss you ever since you came back."

He squeezed her breasts together, and she shivered in his arms.

"Nathan," Janice said, only able to breathe his name in the softest of breaths.

"You're so sexy. You smell so damn good." He punctuated the words with moist kisses along her neck and sucked on her full lower lip. "You torture me every single day. Tell me you want this."

Janice let her tongue touch his, retreat, then surge forward again, tasting deeper into his mouth. "I do. I want this. I want you."

Nathan pressed his mouth hard to hers and lifted his head. His heavy-lidded gaze met hers.

"Strip for me."

10

Janice curled her fingers into Nathan's shirt, kissed his ear, and sucked on the lobe. Then she dragged her teeth along the underside of his jaw—a move she knew would drive him crazy, and it did. He groaned and caught her blouse in his fists, but she quickly twisted away from him to make her own moves.

Keeping eye contact, she dragged the silk garment over her head with a smooth lift and unhooked her skirt, so it fell around her ankles. She stood before him in a black demi-cup bra and matching lace panties, feeling confident as his hungry gaze ate up every inch of her exposed bronze-colored flesh.

"Look at you," he whispered huskily.

As his gaze swept over her high breasts, he moved slowly forward and licked his lips, backing her toward the desk without touching by walking slowly forward as his eyes swept her figure.

Lifting her hand to his lips, he kissed the tattooed words on her wrist and flicked his tongue across the sensitive skin. The tiny shivers the caress evoked made him laugh softly, an indulgent yet cocky expression taking hold of his features.

His warm hands closed around her breasts and pushed them higher to his bent head. He licked along her cleavage and the crests of her breasts as if he were kissing her lips and made warm shivers run along her skin the entire time.

Moaning and letting her head fall back, Janice lifted her body to him as it came alive in a flare of heat and desire she hadn't experienced with anyone else since the last time they made love.

Nathan popped the front clasp on her bra, and she gasped as the skin tightened and peaked in the cool air. As the garment slid down her arms to the floor, he caught her nipple in his mouth, and she almost collapsed. The sensation of his tongue circling the hard peak and torturing it with firm flicks was almost more than she could bear.

Anxious for a chance to touch bare skin and make him squirm too, Janice tugged at his shirt. He stepped back and quickly removed it and the undershirt, tossing them to the floor and exposing the tattoos on his left arm as well as the beauty of a muscular torso that dipped to a narrow waist right above his waistband.

He came at her again, claiming her mouth, this time with more demand in his touch. As his thick fingers traced the edge of her panties, her body screamed for more, and she whimpered in his mouth.

"Touch me," she begged, angling her pelvis to force the direct contact.

She had no willpower where Nathan was concerned. No reservations. She simply ached for the pleasure she knew he could give.

"Like this?" he whispered.

One hand slid down under the lace from behind, gliding over the curve of her bottom to finger her core with a possessive touch.

"Yes." She panted the word and leaned into him, sighing in bliss at all the sensations she experienced in his arms.

His hands and mouth took full control of her body, and she turned into nothing but a slave to his touch. The hairs on his bare chest tickled her nipples. His moist mouth on her neck sent a cacophony of sensation exploding beneath her skin. The hand down her panties squeezed her butt and then glided further to play in the wetness that saturated her delicate underthings.

Surrounded by his touch, she experienced unspeakable pleasure that kept her practically immobile—moaning, breathing heavy, and bending to his will.

But that wasn't enough for Nathan. He put his other hand down the front of her underwear and with brutal accuracy, captured her clit between two fingers. From the front and behind, he tortured her body. His fingers slid back and forth between her swollen lips, while his other hand gripped and squeezed her fleshy behind.

When the two digits entered her heat, Janice lost control and cried out with complete abandon. Her cries sounded like alarm bells in the quiet office, but she couldn't stop the sounds. She came so hard it took her breath away. She spasmed around his fingers and squeezed her eyes shut, gripping his shoulders, puffs of air hitting his chest as she thrust her hips hard to keep up with the rhythm of his hands.

When her breathing finally normalized, she came back to reality with her head against Nathan's chest. His fingers had left her core, and his other hand rubbed gently up and down the curve in her spine.

Janice lifted her head and met his gaze. She knew he wasn't finished. He had only just begun.

"Turn around."

Her breath hitched in anticipation, and she did as he

commanded. She couldn't wait to find out what he had planned for the next phase of their lovemaking.

"I love everything about your body," Nathan whispered in a rough-textured voice. "Your neck." He lifted her hair and kissed the back of her neck. "Your breasts." His hands slid forward across her ribs and upward to cup her breasts. "Everything." He kissed the middle of her shoulder blades. "Bend over."

Janice could hardly breathe as she bent over the desk, arching her back and lifting onto her toes as Nathan dragged his hands down the middle of her spine. His hands moved lower and slid to the lacy panties and ever so slowly pushed them off her hips.

"Step out," he said, and she did as he asked. "Now be a good girl and spread your legs open."

She eased her legs wider, and her body quivered in that position. She felt so exposed, so vulnerable, lying with her breasts pressed into the cool desk, naked in his office with only heels on and her legs open, waiting for him to act.

"I want a quick taste before I fuck you."

Her legs began to shake. In the reflection of the window, she saw him crouch down behind her.

His hands gripped her ass and squeezed and rubbed each cheek. They roughly pushed her bottom higher and further exposed her wet core for the attack of his mouth.

She let out a soft cry, and her nails scraped the cherrywood as he kissed her swollen lower lips and licked at her clit.

Dear god that felt good.

"Nathan," she whimpered.

"I missed this." He growled the heated words almost angrily against her flesh.

He forced one of her knees onto the desk and angled his head in a bid to get more—licking and sucking and taking his fill.

He was unstoppable, absolutely relentless, bound and

determined to do as he pleased. He feasted like he never intended to stop, and all she could do was take what he offered and revel in the pleasure of his forceful hands and wicked mouth. When he hummed against her tender flesh, she teetered on the cusp of a pending orgasm.

But he didn't let her come. With one final lip smack, Nathan stood upright and then slapped her hard on the ass.

"I can't wait to be inside you."

Janice let her leg slide back to the floor and listened to the sounds of his undressing fill the silence in the room. The jingle of his belt and the drag of the zipper held an ominous promise she couldn't wait to receive.

She looked back in time to see him sheathe himself in latex.

"You ready, sweetheart?" Nathan asked.

"Yes." Her voice quivered with longing. She'd never been so ready in her whole entire life.

Nathan leaned over and licked the side of her neck and with one fluid movement, slid inside her core. The reuniting of their bodies brought indescribable pleasure. He kept his legs on the outside of hers and forced her thighs into a tight squeeze. As if that wasn't enough, he grasped her breasts and squeezed them together as his rhythmic thrusts increased in tempo.

Perched on her toes with her bottom in the air and hands splayed out on the wooden surface of the desk, Janice kept time with the sensual rhythm of his undulating hips. She knew she wouldn't last long. She felt the fullness of his girth with deep awareness and experienced greater friction through her pressed-together thighs.

Moaning and whimpering, she let her cheek touch the desk and listened to the sounds of his masculine grunts as he worked his hips.

Her second orgasm didn't take long to appear. Not after such thorough prepping from his mouth, and certainly not with his hands squeezing her aroused breasts and the thickness of his erection sliding in and out of her wet core.

The climax spiraled through her body with the force of a twister, and she let out a fierce cry. Her thighs trembled, and her eyes squeezed shut as she listened to his heavy panting and absorbed the punishing thrusts that signaled his pending orgasm.

She came again. This time with body shaking, ass-clenching shivers that pummeled her insides as his deep strokes drove her farther from sanity and deeper into mind-blowing paradise.

Nathan finally came, too. With a guttural shout, his fingers tightened on her sensitive breasts, and his body stiffened like a plank of hardwood as he joined her in the delicious throes of ecstasy.

THE ROOM WAS QUIET, now that all the panting and groaning had stopped. They were both completely naked, wearing neither clothes nor shoes. Nathan lay on his back with Janice on top of him, her cheek resting on his chest. The sex was great, but it also felt good to simply hold her again.

He trailed his palm repeatedly from the middle of her back down to her cushy behind.

"I was not expecting this. I came in here to share a drink with you and apologize," Janice said softly.

"But then you decided to seduce me?" he teased.

"That's not quite what happened," she said with a soft laugh.

They remained silent for a bit, simply enjoying each other's company and the gratification that came from skin-to-skin contact.

"I never told you the reason Sherilyn gave for not accepting my proposal."

Janice tensed. "What was the reason?"

"She said I was still in love with my coworker."

She looked up at him, lips parted in shock. "You talked about me to her?"

"Only a few times that I can remember, but what I said must have made quite an impression because she guessed that I still had feelings for you. She suggested that we split up until I addressed my unresolved feelings. My immediate thought was to deny what she said and tell her she was wrong, but pretty quickly, I had to admit that she was right. I've been fighting my feelings ever since you came back, and it's been hard as hell."

Janice's gaze lowered, hiding her reaction to his words.

Nathan brushed the hair from her forehead. "Don't over-think what's happening between us."

She looked up at him. "I'm not."

"I know you, and if you aren't now, you will. You'll come up with a million different reasons why we shouldn't be together when all that matters is that you want me as much as I want you." He squeezed her soft bottom.

He turned onto his side so that she was sandwiched between him and the back of the sofa and pinched her chin between his thumb and forefinger. "We can take things slow, and we don't have to make any promises to each other yet. We'll do casual for now and take our time and get to know each other again on a personal level. And when you're ready, we'll talk about the more serious aspects of a relationship."

"Like what?" she asked in a whisper.

"Like marriage."

She bit her bottom lip but didn't appear opposed to the idea, which was a good sign.

"For now, let's enjoy what we have because I can't imagine going back to simply being coworkers. Can you?"

"No, I can't. I don't want to," she admitted.

That was a hell of an admission coming from a woman who remained reserved in her relationships. Thoroughly satisfied, Nathan played with her nipple, not sucking or licking, just brushing his lips across the tip.

"It drives me crazy when you do that," she said huskily.

"I know." He flicked his tongue across the tips of each breast.

Janice groaned, and that was his signal to cover her mouth in a deep kiss. He loved her, and he believed she loved him too, and eventually, they'd figure out how to make their relationship work. He'd make sure of it because he couldn't go back to the cool interactions they had before tonight.

They made love in slow motion with teasing kisses and slow, gentle caresses. When she was wet and practically begging for his possession, Nathan sealed their bodies with a languid stroke.

Her head fell back as his hips thrust between her thighs. He knew when she came because of the soft, patchy cries that filled the air and the erotic sensation of her nails sinking into the muscles of his back.

That's when he allowed himself to let go, and with the hard groan of a satisfied man, emptied his body into bliss.

11

"I found a gray hair," Janice said, touching a spot on Nathan's head.

"Thanks," he said dryly.

They had come back to bed and were watching the national news after a filling breakfast of bacon, eggs, and French toast, all of which had been prepared by Nathan and Adam. Nathan allowed her to pour the orange juice and nothing else because he knew her skills did not reside in the kitchen.

"I like your premature gray hairs. They add character." Janice flung an arm across his chest.

"Is that the best you can do after you insult me?"

Giggling, she glanced up at him. "How did I insult you?"

"How would you like if I find all the gray hairs on your head?" A wicked smile crossed his luscious lips, and he eyed her rumpled hair.

"Don't. You. Dare."

"So you admit you have some?"

"I don't know, but I'd rather not find out at the moment. So don't go searching for any."

"I thought they added...oh, what was the word...character?"

"They do. For you, not me."

Nathan flipped her over onto her back and slid a hard thigh between hers. "Oh, really?" He kissed her neck, and she arched her throat into the sensation of his soft lips. "I don't care if you have a head full of gray hairs. You're still the sexiest woman I've ever known," he whispered.

Janice cupped the back of his head and moaned. "You always say the sweetest thing."

He looked deeply into her eyes. "Those aren't just words, Janice. I mean them." He tracked his fingers through her hair.

"Anyone ever tell you you're an amazing man?"

"All the time."

She laughed and slapped his shoulder. "I'm serious. You really are."

"So you actually believe that now?" he asked.

"I'm still working on my...fears, if that's what you want to call it. But yes, I believe that you're a good man. I always knew you were."

Nathan traced the outer edge of her lips with his index finger. "And you are an amazing woman."

As he lowered his head to kiss her, her phone on the night-stand rang. The unique ring tone was the one assigned to Reynolds Construction.

Janice groaned.

"Ignore it."

"I can't. It's my contractor."

He frowned and rolled off her. "A contractor shouldn't elicit that type of response."

"Unfortunately, mine does." Taking a deep breath, she picked up the phone and answered the call. "Hi, Mr. Reynolds. What's the latest?"

She settled against the pillows with her back to the headboard.

"I hate to do this to you, darling, but I won't have those

quotes ready, and I have to put off your project for about a month."

"A month!" Janice sat up in alarm, one arm holding the sheet against her chest. "What's wrong now?"

"I have a family emergency that's going to take me out of town. I promise, when I come back I'll double-time it so we can get your house completed in a timely fashion."

"Mr. Reynolds, this is going to cause serious problems for me."

"I'll make it up to you when I get back into town. Don't worry your pretty little head about a thing, okay? If I can get back sooner, I'll let you know."

Janice gritted her teeth. She was tired of him putting her off and tired of him telling her not to "worry her pretty little head about a thing."

"All right, I'll talk to you when you get back."

They hung up, and Janice fell back against the pillows.

"What happened?"

Janice told him everything Reynolds said, and when she finished, Nathan didn't look pleased. In fact, he seemed rather angry. "What kind of family emergency requires him to take a month off, and why didn't he at least have the quotes like he promised?"

"I don't know, he didn't say. With him, it's not a matter of if something is going to happen, but when. This man came highly recommended, and he's been a problem the entire time."

"Guarantee you he bid on another job and is going to work on it. That's the family emergency."

"Don't say that," Janice said with a groan, though she'd thought the same.

"If you're interested, I have a friend who used to be the foreman for a builder. Now he has his own construction company. He's on the higher side but has a great reputation, and I trust him. Let him take a look at the house and see how long it would take to finish the work you have left."

The idea appealed to Janice. And to be honest, she had lost trust in Reynolds Construction.

"Okay, I'll talk to him. That said, I'm not making any promises that I'll hire him. Jada gave me the name of a guy, too, and I want to check him out."

"Fair enough. But once you talk to my guy and meet him, I promise you'll want to work with him. He's good people."

He picked up his phone from the side table and dialed a number.

"What's his name?" Janice whispered.

"Tomas."

"Tomas Molina?"

"Yeah. You know him?"

"That's Jada's guy. Since you both recommend him, that must be a good sign."

A few seconds later, Janice was on the phone with a man with an accent. He promised to meet them at the property in the afternoon after he completed another estimate.

After she hung up, she turned to Nathan. "Thank you so much. You're coming with me, I hope?"

"Of course. But I have some work to do before we go over there," he said, his voice a low grumble.

"What work?" Janice asked, grinning, her body already getting warm with anticipation.

Nathan dragged away the sheet to reveal her nakedness. "Let me show you."

Then he went to work.

～

TOMAS MOLINA MET Janice and Nathan at the house at the

appointed time. That alone impressed Janice, but his friendly demeanor also put her at ease.

He was a tall Cuban with a brawny physique that hinted at his years in the construction field, and brown hair with natural blond highlights pulled back into a ponytail.

He nodded at Nathan, and both men shook hands. "How have you been?"

"Can't complain. Yourself?" Nathan asked.

"Can't complain, either. It's summertime, our busiest time of the year." He directed a smile at Janice that she might have misinterpreted as flirtatious if she didn't notice the ring on his left hand. "Tomas Molina. Nice to meet you."

"Janice Livingston. Nice to meet you." His big hands bore the rough texture of a laborer.

As they strolled through the house, he asked questions about her plans and took notes in a small pad he removed from his back pocket. In addition, he used some kind of laser tool to take measurements.

He was very professional, and though he didn't utter a negative word, she had the distinct impression he was disturbed by her explanation of the delays and additional costs she'd experienced. Nathan remained behind them, interjecting twice with questions, but letting her take the lead in the conversation with Tomas.

In the fenced-in backyard, Janice explained her landscaping ideas and showed Tomas photographs on her phone of what she wanted to implement.

"How long do you think it would take you to finish the work?" she finally asked.

"Based on what I see, we can have the renovations completed in six weeks, sixty days at the latest."

"Including the landscaping?" Janice asked, surprised.

"Everything."

"What about the crumbling foundation and electrical issues?"

He frowned. "I didn't see any foundation issues. And what I can do, if you'll allow me, is come back out here and do a more thorough inspection with my electrician to be sure about the wiring. Do you have a write-up of the problems the other contractor told you about?"

"Yes. He sent it by email."

"Forward the details to me, including the rest of your ideas, any photos you have, and I'll send an estimate by the middle of next week. And if you don't mind, I'll need the lockbox code to get back into the house to do a more thorough inspection. But like I said, I don't see the major issues he stated."

"I don't mind giving you the code at all. As a matter of fact, can I ask you something else?"

"Sure."

"I want to get some custom cabinets done. The price I was quoted was much higher than I anticipated, but because I don't know much about these things, the contractor assured me that it was reasonable. Do you know anyone who does custom work and could give me an estimate on having the cabinets done?"

"Absolutely. A good friend of mine does that type of work. That's all he does." Tomas pulled out his wallet and removed two cards. "Here's my card, and the second one belongs to Ryan Stewart, my friend who does custom furniture. You can reach him at the shop number during the day unless he has a delivery. Give him a call and let him know what you're looking for, and when I come out here, I'll have him meet me to do the measurements. I'll send everything to you in one estimate."

The weight of a boulder had been lifted off her shoulders. She had a good feeling about this man. "That would be great. Thank you so much."

"Not a problem. Well, I'll get going. I'm supposed to meet

my wife and some friends for dinner, and I need to get cleaned up." He shook her hand and then shook Nathan's. "Thanks."

"No problem. I know you'll take good care of her," Nathan said.

"Of course." Tomas grinned and then walked back into the house.

"Well, what do you think?" Nathan asked.

Janice hadn't realized what a burden working with Reynolds Construction had been. She felt a lot better already.

"Thank you. And don't look so smug."

He pulled her into his embrace. "You know how I hate to be right."

She smiled up at him. "Yes, I know. But you're not right yet. I have to see how he works first."

"He'll work out fine, and then you can apologize to Jada."

"Ugh. She's probably going to gloat like you."

"And rightly so. You could have saved yourself a lot of headaches if you'd listened to her in the first place. Come on, I'll let you buy me lunch as a thank-you."

"Oh, goody."

They both laughed on the way inside the house.

12

"Sherilyn, what are you doing here?" Nathan stood in the open doorway of his condo, staring at Sherilyn, who was holding a glass dish covered in aluminum foil.

"I brought you something." Her wide, friendly smile caused a twinge of guilt since they'd only broken up a few weeks ago and he'd hardly thought of her because he was preoccupied with Janice.

He stepped into the hallway and closed the door behind him. He couldn't risk having her enter while Janice was in there. Right now, she was in the shower, so he had time to get rid of Sherilyn.

"Um, I can't come in?" Her searching eyes glanced at the closed door in confusion.

"It's...listen, it's not a good time. I have a guest."

"A female guest?" she asked lightly.

He debated whether or not he should lie, but settled on honesty. "Yes."

"Oh." The one-syllable word was spoken quietly, but she was clearly surprised. "Well, here I was feeling guilty because I turned down your proposal. I brought by a peach cobbler as a peace offering because I know how much you and Abram like my cobblers, but you've already bounced back."

"Sherilyn—"

"Anyone I know?"

Here is where he had to lie because according to Sherilyn, though he only recalled mentioning Janice to her a couple of times, he was still in love with her. And she had been right.

"No. No one you know." Technically, she and Janice *didn't* know each other.

"That's why you didn't push back when I turned you down and suggested we go our separate ways. I kept waiting for you to call and prove me wrong. You were probably relieved because you already had someone else."

"*No.* I didn't push back because you were right. We didn't belong together."

"I feel so silly for coming here," she said with downcast eyes, her voice trembling.

Nathan stepped closer but refrained from touching her. "Don't. Bringing by the cobbler was very thoughtful of you."

She gazed at him. "I care about you. I just didn't believe you cared about me in the same way."

She was right, and turning him down had saved them both pain and heartache that would certainly come later.

"I'm here, so take it. If not for you, for Abram."

Nathan took the dish. "I'll enjoy it, too. Thanks. We'll return the dish as soon as we're finished."

Sherilyn stepped back and shook her head vigorously. "Keep it. The way you did my heart."

Oh, shit.

"You deserve more than I offered. I did and still do care about you, but you were right, marriage wasn't the right move for us, and I'm glad we had that talk."

When relationships end and feelings are hurt, the injured party doesn't want to hear about why they deserve more than the other person was willing to give. It always sounded cliché or insincere. Nonetheless, Nathan felt compelled to say the words because they were true, and he hoped the veracity of his words came through.

"Me too. Good talk. I hope you've found someone to help you forget her. Enjoy the cobbler."

Sherilyn walked away with a stiff back and her head held high.

When she'd disappeared out of sight, Nathan slipped back inside and encountered Janice coming from the kitchen. She wore one of his white undershirts over a pair of bright pink yoga pants.

"I was looking for you. What's that?" She arched a brow. She didn't have on a stitch of makeup, her hair was a messy tumble of uncombed curls, and she'd never looked lovelier.

"Peach cobbler."

"What store delivers peach cobbler covered in aluminum foil?" she asked in an amused voice.

"Not a store. Sherilyn brought it by." Nathan watched closely for her reaction.

The smile fell off Janice's face.

He set down the cobbler and grasped her upper arms. "It's not a red flag. She brought the cobbler as a nice gesture because she feels guilty about turning down my proposal and saying we should split up. I told her I had a guest, and she left. This is probably the last I'll see of her, and if she comes around again, I'll make it clear she can't anymore. But she won't."

"You're sure?"

He looked deeply into her eyes. "I can't be one hundred percent certain, but I'm pretty sure. If she does, I'll deal with it."

Nathan pulled her into his arms and closed his arms around her soft body. She smelled like the berry body wash she used in the shower. The scent made the bathroom smell like a field of strawberries. *She* smelled like a field of strawberries.

He nuzzled behind her ear. "You smell good." He kissed her neck, and her body relaxed against him.

Her arms circled his torso, and he threaded his fingers into her thick hair and forced her head back at an angle so he could look down into her brown eyes. "No drama."

"Promise?"

He shouldn't promise, but what else could he say?

"I promise."

JANICE ENTERED NATHAN'S BEDROOM. He was still fast asleep because it was very early on Saturday morning, and when he didn't have to go to work, Nathan liked to sleep late. She'd spent a lot of time at his condo the past few weeks, and last night after the conversation about Sherilyn and the cobbler, they'd fallen asleep on the sofa watching a movie before she nudged him awake and they made their way back to his room.

Now, however, she was ready for him to wake up. She had big plans for them today.

She climbed on top of him, straddled his hips, and kissed his shoulder and then his neck. "Nathan, wake up."

Nathan groaned and without opening his eyes, dragged a pillow over his head.

"Nathan." Janice yanked away the pillow and tossed it lower on the bed.

"Go away, woman."

"I can't. I need you to wake up. Pretty please."

He opened his eyes to slits and frowned up at her.

"Guess what?" Janice said.

"What's that on your face?"

"Oh, you mean my new glasses? You like?"

She tilted her head to the left and the right so he'd have a good view from both angles. The new glasses consisted of round yellow lenses encircled by a white frame, where the top morphed into white petaled daisies along the top as part of the design. The glasses took up half her face and didn't actually have a prescription in them, so they were only for fun.

Nathan squinted at her. "They're...different."

"I wanted something with a little more pizzazz. A little more zazzoo, if you will."

"Zazzoo is not a word," he pointed out.

"It is now," Janice said.

Nathan sniffed the air. Then he sat up suddenly, eyes wide. "What's burning?"

"Calm down." Janice pressed a hand to his bare chest and forced him onto his back. "I was in the kitchen—"

"What were you doing in the kitchen? You don't cook."

Her good mood drained away. "Sorry I don't bake cobblers from scratch and hand-deliver them."

She moved to get up off Nathan, but before she could, he rolled her onto her back and settled over her on one arm.

"Tell me you're not jealous," he said.

"I'm not jealous." She didn't mean it.

Nathan removed the funky glasses and set them on the bed. "I love you the way you are. You don't have to change."

"I wanted to do something nice for you and Abram. I keep wondering, what do I bring to the table?" Janice said in a small voice. Her failed attempt at cooking had ended with burned pancakes and bacon.

"How could you even ask that? If I wanted someone to cook for Abram and me, I could hire a cook to fill that role. I can't hire someone to fill the role that you do as my lover, my friend, and the person who makes me laugh the most and gets me out of my comfort zone. We're good, you and me. Okay?"

Janice moved her thumb over the stubble on his jaw. "Okay. I won't try cooking again," she said with an embarrassed smile.

"Good."

"Wrong answer."

"I mean... Okay. Wait a minute, what's the right answer?" Janice rolled her eyes, and Nathan chuckled.

He repositioned on the bed so he rested on a nest of pillows against the black leather headboard. "Now, what was it that you wanted me to guess?"

Excited once again, Janice sat cross-legged on the bed facing him. "I want to go for a ride. With you." She tapped the middle of his chest.

Nathan glanced at the digital clock on the table beside his bed. "You mean later? It's seven a.m."

"Which is the perfect time for riding. You know I like to go early in the morning, especially when I have a long trip planned. When was the last time you did the North Atlanta lake loop?""

He ran a hand down his face. "The last time I did that was with you. I haven't been on many long-distance rides. Usually, I only take the Harley out on the weekend to run around town."

"Blasphemy! The Road King was made for the open road, so a long ride is well overdue. Let's hit the road like we used to."

His gaze softened with affection. "When did you get this idea?"

"This morning, when I woke up."

"I'm awake now, but I'll have to see about Abram. He's probably still asleep."

"He was up playing video games and saw my spectacular fail at making breakfast. I mentioned the trip to him, and he said he'd happily stay here and then go hang out with his friends at the mall later."

"Kids still do that?"

"Apparently. So, are you definitely coming? I'll sweeten the deal with some hot sex." She bounced her eyebrows up and down.

"I could have hot sex anytime I want."

"Oh, you can?"

"You know I can," Nathan said confidently, lowering his voice. His eyes skimmed over her bare arms in the tank top and made her skin wake up with goose bumps.

Moving quickly, he rolled her onto her back. One hand slid between her legs and possessively cupped her sex, and she let out an involuntary moan.

While his hand caressed her with languid strokes until she was wet and achy, Nathan pressed his lips to her neck and sucked on the tender skin. "You were saying?"

"Maybe a quickie," Janice murmured.

When he gently squeezed her damp sex, she gasped and arched her back.

"Why don't we kill two birds with one stone? Join me in the shower," he whispered huskily.

"Mr. Crenshaw, I like that idea."

They tumbled out of bed, and Janice scampered into the en suite bathroom with Nathan close behind.

HANDS ON HER HIPS, Janice surveyed Nathan in his building's garage. She'd forgotten how delicious he looked wearing knee pads over jeans, gloves, and a leather vest over a black shirt that showed off his cut arms.

"You look soooo sexy," she gushed, running a finger down his tattooed left arm.

"You look sexier." He dropped a kiss on her lips.

She licked her mouth and savored his taste. His easy affection buoyed her spirits and was a balm to her worrying heart.

She caught the front of his vest and stepped into him. "Thank you."

"For what?"

"For what you said earlier, about not wanting me to change."

Nathan tilted up her chin. "I was miserable without you, and I'm glad you're back in my life, so it's for purely selfish reasons that I say don't change. I meant what I said, sweetheart. I love you the way you are."

Janice raised up on her toes and gave him a kiss, flicking her tongue across his lips. "I love you the way you are, too." She dropped back onto her feet. "Ready?" She pulled on her gloves.

"Yes, ma'am."

Nathan smacked her on the booty, and she let out a little squeal before slapping away his hand. With a warm, masculine chuckle, he swung one long leg over the Road King and revved the engine.

They pulled out of the garage, and the motors of the powerful Harleys filled the air around them.

The North Atlanta lake run was a four-hour ride that included Lake Allatoona, Lake Lanier, and took them into the downtown of smaller cities like Cartersville and Cumming. They alternated taking the lead and other times rode side by side down the picturesque roadways.

For Janice, having Nathan by her side made the lake run the best ride she'd had in a long time.

13

It was the kind of watch he'd like.

With a black calf leather strap and black and silver design, the Maurice Lacroix timepiece wasn't flashy and represented elegance and style like the man Janice wanted to purchase it for.

"You like it?" she asked Soul.

Her friend had met her at the jeweler after work to take a look at the watch because Janice wanted another opinion.

"I like it, but more importantly, do you think Nathan will like it?"

"I do. The watch fits his personality."

"Then get it."

Nathan's fortieth birthday was coming up in a couple of weeks, and Janice wanted to give him a gift that let him know in no uncertain terms exactly how much he meant to her. She wanted to demonstrate that she'd grown and understood they were in a different relationship than before and that she didn't view him through the same lens she had viewed other men. He was special, she was ready to take the emotional leap she'd been afraid to take before, and she wanted him to know that.

She looked at the saleswoman. "Let's put the engraving on this one."

"Good choice," the woman said in a hushed tone. She handed the watch to a young man who took it and went into a back room.

Janice took care of the payment, and while they waited, she and Soul talked, keeping their voices low to match the atmosphere in the store.

"Thanks for meeting me," Janice said, perusing the bracelets in one of the showcases.

"Of course. I'm sure Nathan will love the watch. You've come a long way." Soul bumped a narrow hip into Janice.

"What do you mean?"

"The fact that you're actually jumping back into a relationship with someone you broke up with before, and you don't seem to have any reservations about it."

"Double-dipping, as Jada would say?" Janice asked in amusement.

Soul gave a little laugh. "Exactly."

She pondered her friend's words. "You know what, I think it's because I've finally accepted that there are no perfect relationships. They certainly don't have to be as dysfunctional as the one my parents had, or as spirit-crushing as having your fiancé run off with his stepmother."

"I still can't believe he did that," Soul said with a shake of her head.

"I do have concerns about how we'll handle problems in the relationship, but what's different is that I accept that everybody has problems. And the concerns I have aren't related to Nathan or his character, you know what I mean?"

Soul nodded. "I do. When you find a good man, hold onto him," she said with heartfelt emphasis. She spoke from experience, as she and her college sweetheart Micah had recently reconciled.

They talked for a little longer, and then the saleswoman returned and showed Janice the engraving on the back.

You are my heart's desire.

A smile filtered across her lips. The engraving embodied everything she wanted Nathan to know. Their relationship was normal, and they had fun, and when they disagreed, they never stayed angry at each other. That had always been the case, but she'd been too foolish to take note and allowed fear to send her running from her blessing.

Nathan represented everything she'd been searching for. He was a good man who loved her unconditionally and treated her the way she wanted to be treated. He was the manifestation of her heart's desire, and she wouldn't allow anyone to take that away from her—not even herself.

"I'd like to have it gift-wrapped," she told the saleswoman.

Afterward, paper sack in hand, she and Soul exited the store. Now all she had to do was make reservations for dinner at Nathan's favorite restaurant, and plans for his fortieth birthday weekend would be complete.

Janice was about to bid goodbye to Soul when her friend stared at the Avalon.

"Oh, no. Look at that." Soul pointed.

Two flat tires.

Janice's mouth fell open. "You have got to be kidding me. What did I do, run over two nails this time?" She walked around to the driver's side and pulled up short. "These are flat, too."

"What?" Soul rushed around the car and gaped at the damage.

They stared at each other.

"What are the chances that I accidentally have four flat tires?"

"You already know the answer. This was no accident. Someone slashed your tires."

Janice looked up and down the street, her eyes searching for anyone who didn't belong or acted oddly, but she didn't see any unusual behavior. Some people had recently left work and were on the way home, while others were on the way to happy hour, and cars cruised by slowly in the heavy traffic.

Everyone looked perfectly normal. No one appeared out of place. Yet the cold hand of fear chilled her to the bone.

∽

"Something's obviously bothering you," Abram said for the second time that night.

"Whatever's bothering me, you're too young to understand."

The scent of cooking meat filled the kitchen.

Friday night burgers had become a ritual with them. They purchased the patties already seasoned, and Nathan cooked them on the stove top grill. While he cooked, Abram laid out the fixings—lettuce, sliced tomatoes, bread, and condiments. Potato salad purchased from a nearby deli was tonight's accompaniment.

"Come on, man. You're always telling me to share what I feel. You encourage me to tell you what's on my mind, but you don't do the same for me."

"Did you not hear what I said? That's because you're too young."

"I'm not too young! I know a lot, and besides, don't you need someone to talk to?"

Nathan carefully placed two slices of cheese on each burger and turned off the heat. Then he set the spatula beside the grill and faced his younger brother.

Before he said a word, Abram said, "Trust me."

Nathan groaned and sighed heavily. "You're not going to stop, are you?"

"No. I get that from you." His round face lit up in a grin.

"Uh-huh. Okay, here's the thing. My relationship with Janice is going really well..." He still wasn't sure he should have this conversation with a sixteen-year-old.

"Are you going to tell me or not?" Abram asked.

"Slow your roll."

"Come on, man." Abram laughed.

"All right, Janice and I are being...how should I say this...? We agreed not to pressure each other and be casual about the relationship. Now I regret it." He already saw Janice as his woman, and as far as he was concerned, they were in a committed relationship, but he didn't know for sure how she viewed their relationship.

"That's all? Just take it back," Abram said simply.

Nathan laughed. "You can't just take it back. That's not the way relationships work."

"Aren't you always telling me about the importance of communication? Blah, blah, blah, use your words. Yada, yada, yada, honest communication is the foundation of all interpersonal relationships."

"Well, at least I know you're listening when I talk," Nathan said dryly.

"You're always beating that crap—I mean, words of wisdom —into my head, so why aren't you following your own advice? Shouldn't you communicate with her?"

"It's not that easy, Abram. We're not only involved romantically, we also have to work with each other."

"Well, maybe you shouldn't have hooked up with her." Abram spoke with heavy solemnity as if he'd said something incredibly profound.

"We've already crossed that bridge," Nathan pointed out.

"Here's the thing, sounds to me like you have the perfect setup. I mean, think about it. If your relationship isn't that serious, when it's all over, you can go back to business as usual. You guys can be grown-ups, not emotional like us young people, right? So what are you complaining about? I'm kind of jealous. I can't do that with Ashley." He snorted.

"You should not be doing that with Ashley or any other girl."

"Why not? You're doing it."

"You ever heard of *do what I say and not what I do*?"

Abram sighed. "Yes," he said wearily.

"That applies here." Nathan frowned. "Are you having sex?"

"No!" Abram's voice came out in a squeak.

"If you are, you better—"

"Wrap it up. Yeah, I know, but I'm not yet, so chill."

Nathan removed the burgers from the grill and placed each one on a bun. Then he and Abram took them with all the fixings in front of the television in the living room.

"So what are you going to do about Janice?" Abram asked, right before he took a bite.

"Nothing for now."

"Sounds like a bad idea to me."

"I don't need advice from a sixteen-year-old."

Abram laughed. "You sure about that?"

Nathan tossed a piece of lettuce at him.

"Hey!"

"Yeah. I'm sure about that."

"Can I tell you something?"

"Of course."

Abram didn't speak right away, and Nathan waited him out. Sometimes Abram took a while to formulate his thoughts. He dug into the potato salad while he waited.

"I like her," Abram said simply.

"Yeah?"

Abram shrugged. "I mean, she's cool. That time we all went bowling was fun, and when you're busy, she talks to me. And she's kinda different from Sherilyn. She's so..." He wiggled and flailed his hands.

Nathan burst out laughing. "What the hell was that?"

Abram grinned, his cheeks turning red. "She's colorful and always in a good mood."

"I'm glad you like her."

"So then you'll figure out how to make it work, right?"

"Yes, for your sake. So you can have a stepmother."

"Thanks, Dad," Abram said with a grin.

They finished eating and were halfway through a movie when Janice let herself in with the spare key Nathan had given her. She had an overnight bag on her shoulder. "Hey, you two," she said.

"Hey, beautiful. How was your day?"

"Nice."

He stood, and she came over and greeted him with a kiss.

"I'm going to get out of here before you guys start acting all lovey-dovey." Abram made kissing sounds.

"You're real funny," Nathan told him.

After he was gone, Nathan studied Janice's expression. "You look like you have something on your mind."

She dropped her bag onto the floor beside the sofa and took a deep breath. "A weird thing happened this afternoon. Soul and I were hanging out downtown, and when we left one of the shops, I saw that I had four flat tires."

"Four flat tires? That's impossible. That sounds like vandalism, sweetheart. Why didn't you call me?"

"Soul stayed with me. I filed a police report, but with no witnesses, there was nothing they could do. The whole ordeal gave me the creeps." She shivered. "I don't understand why anyone would do that. It was so random."

The minute the words left her mouth, Sherilyn came to mind.

"Maybe the situation isn't so random," Nathan said slowly.

"You think I was specifically targeted? By who?" A thread of panic filled her voice.

"I'm not sure, but maybe…my ex, Sherilyn."

Her eyes widened. "Does she know me?"

"She didn't before, but it would be easy enough for her to figure out who you are, and she gets a kick out of doing investigative work—as she calls it—since she works for a P.I. I'm not saying it's definitely her, but I can't say it's not, either. Like I told you before, she turned down my proposal because she suspected I still had feelings for you. If she somehow found out you and I are together, and you were my guest the night she came over, she might not be too happy."

Janice folded her arms over her chest and paced the floor. "I don't like this. This is exactly the kind of foolishness I want to avoid."

"I'll talk to her and make sure she stays far away from you."

She stopped moving. "No. If you're right and Sherilyn is jealous of me, that might make her jealousy worse. Has she been in touch since she dropped off the cobbler?"

"No."

"Then let's leave her alone for now. We don't know she slashed the tires. It could have been kids, for all we know, and we're jumping to conclusions."

"Are you sure?" While he agreed that they didn't know for sure, he wondered if he shouldn't issue some kind of warning to his ex, as a precautionary measure.

"I'm fine. Nothing happened except I was inconvenienced and out some money because of the tires. I say we leave well enough alone."

He took her hand. "If any other strange happenings take place, make sure you call me."

"I will."

Nathan wasn't completely satisfied, but he didn't want to cause undue alarm because Janice was right. They had no proof Sherilyn had vandalized her car. If she didn't, then the incident was a one-time occurrence they never had to worry about again. If she did, he knew without a doubt that there was more to come.

He hoped like hell the former was correct.

14

With laughter touching their lips, Nathan and Janice strolled out of the restaurant hand-in-hand, in between a group of twelve friends. The group, which included Janice's two roommates, had joined them for dinner at his favorite restaurant. He was having a wonderful fortieth-birthday celebration because he was spending it with friends, and more importantly, the woman he loved.

Janice wore a halter top dress covered in pink, blue, and red flowers. A red satin sash enveloped her waist and tied in the back. Her thick red hair was pulled up into a textured twist he couldn't wait to unravel once he got her pretty ass home.

"Good night, Nathan! Happy birthday!" one of the female guests called, blowing drunken kisses at him until her husband hauled her away.

"Janice, we'll see you at home, or not," Soul said. Giggling, she and Jada hopped into the waiting Uber.

Their other friends waited for their cars to arrive or had parked in a public lot, and he and Janice exchanged hugs with them before walking away to go to the parking lot where he'd left his vehicle.

"I think half our friends are drunk," Nathan remarked.

"I think so, too. At the very least, tipsy."

He swung an arm around her neck and squeezed her close. He bent his lips to her ear. "I had a blast, sweetheart. Thank you."

"You're welcome, but there's more."

"There's more?" he repeated with a leer.

"Not *that*, although you'll get that later, too."

She looked so happy, her face bright and cheerful, the perfect accompaniment to the bright-colored clothing she wore. If he did nothing for the rest of his days but sit back and watch her, he'd be perfectly content. All her funky glasses were quirky but cool. The colorful clothes were loud yet comforting. She was sexy, with great breasts and a contagious laugh that made him never want to leave her side. He was convinced no one could be in a bad mood in her presence.

"I have a confession to make. Do you remember when I started at The Winthrop?" he asked.

"Vaguely."

"I remember it vividly. I started in the fall on a day rain was pouring down. You came rushing into the lower lobby with a plain old black umbrella—surprisingly—but a bright red coat, which is more you."

"I remember that coat. And I remember that day."

They took their time strolling along, bodies resting against each other.

"I didn't know you, and you didn't know me, so we couldn't have said more than two words to each other at the time. But from the moment I saw you, I knew I wanted you, and nothing would get in my way."

Her arm tightened around his torso as she gazed up at him. "That's not a confession. That's a declaration of war."

"Not war. A declaration of interest."

"Do you always get whatever you're interested in?"

"Always. Took me longer than usual this time, and I almost messed up by moving on with someone else."

Nathan stopped in the middle of the sidewalk, cupped her face, and gave her a deep, heartfelt kiss. If there was any pleasure he never wanted to live without, it was the opportunity to kiss Janice Livingston at will.

"Let's get you home, birthday boy." She breathed the words against his lips, stirring his loins with the promise of what was to come later.

"Yes, ma'am."

Holding hands, they walked across the street to the uncovered parking lot where he'd left the SUV and waved at the attendant in the booth as they went by. The Mercedes was in the back corner. As they approached, a red Sentra pulled out of its parking space, and Nathan had an unobstructed view of the passenger side of his vehicle. What he saw made both his and Janice's footsteps crawl to a halt.

Her mouth fell open. Nathan, for his part, couldn't believe his eyes.

LIAR, in all caps, had been spray-painted on the side in vivid red letters over the electric blue finish.

Nathan released Janice and walked slowly around to the driver's side. The same word was emblazoned there as well.

Fury bellowed inside of him.

Standing a few feet from the front of the Mercedes, Janice shook her head in disbelief. "Do you think Sherilyn did this, too?"

"I don't doubt she did for one minute. I noticed she had a dramatic side, but to slash your tires and spray-paint my car..." He couldn't finish the sentence because anger consumed him.

Not only did the vandalism upset him, but the fact that she'd clearly followed them like a damn stalker.

"I'm calling the police." He pulled out his phone.

"You'll never be able to prove she did this," Janice said.

"There have to be cameras around here somewhere, and we're in an almost-filled parking lot in the middle of Atlanta on a Friday night. Someone must have seen her or her car. I'm going to demand a full investigation and ride their asses until they get enough for her to be charged."

Nathan dialed the nonemergency number for the police, and when the operator came on the line, he explained that a crime had already taken place and he needed to make a report. To expend his angry energy, he walked back and forth as he answered questions about their location.

"You're wasting your time," a female voice said.

The voice did *not* belong to Janice.

Nathan spun around.

Sherilyn stood away from them with her hands stuffed into the pockets of her denim jacket. She looked ready for battle with her legs spread shoulder-width apart, no makeup, and her hair bound back from her face.

"Sherilyn, what the hell do you think you're doing?" Nathan started toward her. "You can't—"

She pulled out one hand and revealed a gun, which she pointed at Janice. "Don't make another move or I'll shoot her."

Nathan stopped moving right away. *Holy shit. Had she lost her fucking mind?*

He twisted his head in Janice's direction and met her panic-stricken eyes.

"Sherilyn, put the gun away." He spoke calmly, though alarm buffeted his insides with fists of steel.

"Hang up the phone. Now."

She didn't raise her voice, but she didn't have to. She held a gun in her hand, and the lethal venom in her eyes was enough to inspire Nathan to act. He moved his thumb over the *Off* button and slowly placed the phone back in his pocket.

"You lied to me." Her voice vibrated with hurt and anger. "When I brought you the peach cobbler, I asked you a question, and you lied to me. *She* was the woman in your apartment, and *she* is the reason you never really loved me. Why did you offer me marriage when you didn't love me?"

Nathan swallowed, mind racing as he contemplated how to get them safely out of this mess. "I'm sorry, I was wrong. At the time, I thought marriage was what I wanted, but when you turned me down, I gained clarity and realized the mistake I was about to make."

She sneered. "Oh, isn't that nice. You realized what a mistake you'd made by pretending to love me." She turned to Janice. "Isn't that nice?"

"I did love you, but not—"

"Answer the question!" she screamed at Janice.

"Yes. Yes, that's nice." Janice's voice trembled, and her gaze remained locked on the gun.

Sherilyn wrinkled her nose and used the muzzle of the gun as a pointer. "What the hell is she wearing? She always looks like a clown. This is what you like?"

Now wasn't the time to mention that he loved the way his woman dressed and thought she looked terrific.

"Sherilyn, your problem is with me. Why don't you let her go so you and I can talk alone."

Her eyes narrowed. "I'm angry, not stupid. You can't sweet-talk your way out of this situation." She kept the gun trained on Janice.

"What's your plan? Any minute now someone could pull up and see you. Right now, you have nothing but a vandalism charge. Do you really want to add attempted murder or worse, murder?"

Janice whimpered, and from his position, he could see her shaking. He ached to put his arms around her shoulders and protect her from the craziness their wonderful night had turned into.

"You know what I don't get? You told me what a piece of shit your father was and how you despised the way he treated your mother and the other women in his life. Yet you're exactly like him."

The words hit as hard as a battering ram to his conscience, and his chest burned with shame. He hadn't set out to hurt Sherilyn, but whether intentional or unintentional, that was the result.

"You're right, and I'm sorry."

She shook her head vigorously. "You've said I'm sorry too many times."

"I *am* sorry." Nathan edged forward, worried he was losing her to her emotions. "Give me a chance to make it up to you."

"I told you I'm angry, not stupid." Her eyes flashed in annoyance.

"Then what do you want? How can I fix the wrong I've done?"

"You can't." She focused on Janice with a shift in her expression, as if she'd made up her mind to do something.

"Don't," Janice said in a thready whisper.

"Sherilyn, look at me." Nathan eased a few inches closer. He didn't want to make any sudden moves that might scare her.

She obliged his request. "I suffered, so you have to suffer, too."

"No!" Right before the bullet dislodged, Nathan raced forward the last few inches and flung his body in front of Janice.

The firearm exploded with a resounding *crack* that split the night air and burning pain mushroomed in his body at the speed of light. At the same time, the distant sound of a siren hit his ears, and a vehicle's front lights flashed across his eyelids as his body crashed hard onto the pavement.

15

It was the worst night of her life, and she couldn't stop thinking about it.

Janice sat in broad daylight in the hospital parking lot sobbing in her car, as if Nathan had been shot five minutes before instead of two nights ago.

He was fine. The bullet had been removed from his side and hadn't hit bone or any organs, but she couldn't get over what he'd done. He'd literally jumped in front of a bullet for her, and she didn't know if that was brave or crazy. The urges to alternately hug and slap him came and went with dizzying frequency, her overactive emotions vacillating between deep appreciation and intense anger at his actions.

She swiped at her wet cheeks and checked the redness of her eyes in the mirror behind the sun visor. Satisfied she looked presentable, she dabbed at her nose with a tissue and then exited the Avalon with a bag containing a change of clothes and toiletries for Nathan.

Sherilyn had been arrested at the scene. Luckily, someone who'd pulled into the lot searching for a parking space saw her fire the gun and ran her down. Two men leaped from the car and kept her subdued until the police arrived minutes later. In addition, Nathan had pretended to hang up his phone, but the operator had remained on the line, and the entire confrontation had been recorded. The tape would serve as evidence in the trial to come.

By the time Janice arrived at his room, she was much calmer. Nathan sat on the edge of the bed in a pair of socks and a hospital gown, underneath which his right side was bandaged.

He smiled when he saw her.

"I brought your clothes." Janice held up the duffel bag.

Behind the curtain that divided the room in two, the soft rumble of his roommate's snores could be heard.

"Where's Abram?" she asked.

Neither she nor Abram had left the hospital the night Nathan was shot. The fear on Abram's face when he showed up at the hospital had hurt her heart. Poor kid had lost both of his parents and looked terrified he might lose his brother, too.

Yesterday morning, after Nathan was safely out of surgery and resting peacefully, she and Abram went back to the condo for a shower and change of clothes, but the teenager insisted she bring him back right away, which she did.

She'd fully expected to see him in the same spot beside Nathan's bed, keeping his big brother company with snarky conversation and the latest trending topics on social media.

"I made him go down to the cafeteria to get something to eat. He wouldn't leave my side."

"He's scared."

"But I'm fine, and he has to eat."

"True." She set the duffel bag on the table beside the bed.

"Janice."

He reached for her, but she pretended not to notice and edged away. "Do you need help getting changed in the bathroom?"

"No," Nathan said in a low voice.

He rose from the bed, wincing as he did so.

"I'll wait out here. Holler if you need me."

He nodded and took the bag into the bathroom without another word.

He's fine. He's fine. She kept repeating the words so she wouldn't forget them.

Abram came back from the cafeteria, and the two of them talked while they waited for Nathan to finish getting ready. The doctor came by to check on him before they left and handed Janice pain medicine prescriptions and instructions on how to clean the wound and other particulars to ensure a speedy recovery.

They left the hospital and filled the prescriptions at a local pharmacy, then rode back to the condo with Abram content to do most of the talking from the back seat. When he fell silent and concentrated on his phone, Janice and Nathan didn't break the quiet in the car.

The past forty-eight hours had sent Janice on a rollercoaster ride of emotions. She dreaded the conversation she needed to have with Nathan when they arrived at his home.

"Here you go."

Janice handed Nathan, seated on the end of the bed, a glass of water and two pain pills. He swallowed the pills, drank all the water, and handed the empty glass to her.

"You should get some rest now. The doctor said plenty of rest so you can heal."

"I can't rest right now. Not when you're upset with me."

Taken aback, she frowned at him. "I'm not upset with you."

"You've hardly looked at me in the past twenty-four hours, and you won't let me touch you. I know I fucked up, I should have told Sherilyn the truth, but how long are you going to stay mad at me?"

Janice walked over to the shelf by the window and set down the glass. "I'm not mad at you. I'm mad at me." She turned to face Nathan, arms crossed over her midsection.

"Why?" He looked genuinely confused.

"Because the reason you got shot is my fault."

"Sweetheart, you lost me. How is any of this your fault?"

"I froze. I couldn't move, I couldn't do anything with that gun pointed at me. I should have done something more than just stand there. I could have run while you distracted her with conversation or, I don't know, do anything other than simply stand there and do *nothing*. Then you wouldn't have had to do what you did, because she wanted to hurt you through me. You almost died, and you almost died trying to save *me*." A crazy woman had almost taken away the love of her life, her heart's desire.

"I didn't almost die."

"Yes, you did! Or the damage could have been worse. The doctor said, half an inch lower and you could have lost a kidney. Yes, you're fine because you were lucky, but you shouldn't have done that. What if I had lost you?" Her voice cracked at the end.

"Come here."

Nathan held out his hand, and she reluctantly went to him. He pulled her between his legs. Janice wanted to stay angry, but being close to him melted away the anger and turned her insides to mush.

Nathan cupped her cheek. "What if I had lost *you*? I couldn't let that happen. You mean too much to me. You shouldn't feel guilty because Sherilyn is the one who created that tense situation, and I simply did what I had to do."

She flung her arms around his neck, and he tensed with a

groan. Selfishly, she wanted to squeeze him tight and never let go, but she eased back because he was probably in a lot of pain.

"Sorry, I forgot."

"It's okay." He kept an arm around her waist.

"I love you." She brushed the hair at his temple with her thumb.

"I know."

She stared at him in silence for a moment and then gently kissed his forehead.

"I never got the chance to give you your birthday gift." She eased out of his arms and retrieved the wrapped watch box from the top drawer of his dresser. He'd given her the drawer to keep some of her clothes in since she slept over so often.

She handed over the gift and remained standing before him.

"This was your birthday present."

"Thank you." He unwrapped the box and smiled at the black and silver timepiece inside. "This is nice, sweetheart."

"It's engraved on the back." She turned it over and showed him the underside.

"Damn," he whispered. He looked up at her. "Thank you."

Janice took one of his hands in both of hers. "Don't ever do anything so foolish again."

"Protect you? I can't promise that I won't. Because you're my heart's desire, too."

She bit her bottom lip. "Can you at least promise no more drama? You didn't quite deliver the first time around."

He chuckled, putting his pretty smile and dimples on display. "I'll do my best."

16

"All set in here?" Janice asked Precious as she walked into the copy room.

Janice was about to make a presentation to the executive team about the volunteer program The Winthrop Hotels rolled out over the past year. The program received a tentative name—The Winthrop Helping Hands, and she had to give them an update and let everyone know whether or not it was a success.

"Almost." Precious stuffed the last pieces of paper into the red folders with the company logo emblazoned on the front.

The two women had made up after Janice and Nathan's relationship became public knowledge. After Nathan was shot, it was impossible to keep their relationship quiet. Human Resources talked to them separately to ensure there was no chance of a harassment suit on the horizon, and after some discussion and analysis of the organizational chart, Janice's position was moved to report directly to the CFO instead.

"All set," Precious said. She stacked the folders in a pile and handed them over to Janice.

"Wish me luck," Janice said.

"Good luck," Precious said, giving her a thumbs-up sign.

With a brisk walk, Janice made her way to the conference room where Nathan, the CFO, Nina Winthrop, her two advisors, and a few other executives had gathered.

"Hello, everyone," she said.

The people in the room murmured a greeting, and she handed a folder to each person seated at the conference table.

Nathan sat closest to her on the right. At the head of the table, in her direct line of vision, was Nina Winthrop. Brown-skinned and with her kinky natural hair pulled back into a bun, she looked young, like someone in her early twenties, but was almost thirty.

Janice began her presentation and pointed out the positives and negatives in The Winthrop Helping Hands Program. Overall, she deemed the trial run a success, but with more tweaking, she believed it had the potential to do even better.

The president signaled for attention with a raised pen. "What evidence do you have to substantiate the high employee morale that you're claiming?"

"I don't have concrete evidence, but based on what the hotel managers and operations have told me, employee morale improved. In fact, they contend that productivity improved, and as you saw in slide ten, customer service scores increased almost across the board."

"And you attribute that to increased employee morale?" asked the CFO. He sounded very skeptical.

"I can answer that," said the head of operations. "What we've seen over the past year is that staff taking the time to do good and engaging in these selfless activities made them feel good about themselves. That translated into a better attitude at work, which then meant greater patience and going the extra mile for our customers."

"Isn't that something they did anyway?" Nina's voice was soft, almost hesitant.

The head of operations answered again. "Yes, but we saw anywhere from a one to three-point increase on average in our customer service surveys."

"That's incredible," said one of the advisors, looking down at the data in the folder.

"What was the effect on the bottom line?" asked the president.

Janice flipped to the appropriate slide and used the pointer on the bar graph. "Aside from the costs of paying for the employee trips and compensating them while they volunteered, the costs are negligible. In fact, we saw a small increase in revenue in the last quarter that we attribute to the increased productivity and the better service that resulted in repeat business in some of the hotels. We fully expect to see that continue and perhaps increase over time."

"In conclusion...?" the CFO prompted.

Janice faced the room. "In conclusion, I believe the pilot program was a success. With the tweaks that the operations team and I have recommended, The Winthrop Helping Hands Program can be even more successful. We recommend rolling it out to the entire company."

The room fell silent, and all eyes turned to Ms. Winthrop. Eyes widening, she seemed startled by the sudden attention, but smiled. "That's great news. I'm glad the program was such a success, and I look forward to seeing it rolled out to the entire company, here and abroad. Janice, everyone, thank you very much for all your hard work on this. This project was very important to me, and I'm happy to see it's a viable one for our company." She sent a grateful smile around the table and then rose from the chair.

Everyone else rose with her.

"I'll review the report and get back to you with a final decision on how to move forward," Nina added.

After saying goodbye, she exited the room with her advisors. Everyone else who remained looked at each other.

"That's it, folks. Now we wait," the president said. She gathered up her folder and left the room.

The others followed, but Nathan remained behind.

"Good job," he said.

"It was actually eye-opening. Who would've thought that giving back could reap such rewards in a for-profit company."

He nodded. "I'm a little surprised myself, but we'll see how all of this works once it's rolled out to the entire company. There might be some regional and country-specific differences we'll have to address, but it seems like Ms. Winthrop had a good idea."

"I'll say so." Janice peeped around Nathan. "You coming over tonight?" she whispered.

"*Definitely*," he said enthusiastically with a sexy grin.

She laughed. He sure knew how to make a woman feel good. "Then I'll see you later."

They exited the room together and went their separate ways.

WITH A PAPER SACK balanced on her hip, Janice opened the door to her beautiful home. When Tomas had finished the renovations, Jada took over and helped her create a modern, colorful décor that suited her specific taste.

She walked across the heated tile floor to an open kitchen that flowed into the den, where teal and white Roman blinds matched the teal and orange pillows scattered across a grouping of sofas and chairs. The modern appliances in the kitchen sparkled, the stove practically untouched, but she promised herself one day she'd learn to cook on it.

"Janice, is that you?" Nathan called from upstairs.

"Yes. What are you doing up there?"

"Come and find out."

She grinned. What was he up to? "I'll be right there."

She set the few groceries that she had purchased in the refrigerator and then ran up the stairs. At the top of the staircase, she came to a halt, gazing down at the rose petals scattered on the floor.

"Nathan?"

No answer.

She walked carefully down the hall, following the trail of flowers that led to the bedroom door.

Inside, Nathan had placed candles all around the room. They flickered in the darkness, providing enough illumination so that she could see him lying on the bed in a pair of slacks with his muscular chest on display, legs crossed, and a rose between his teeth.

She giggled. "What are you doing?"

He took the rose from his teeth and swung his legs onto the floor. "I have a cramp in my cheeks. I've been laying there for hours with that thing in my mouth."

She laughed again and shook her head. "You're a terrible liar."

His eyes softened on her, and her chest swelled with happiness. Not once had she grown tired of that look of adoration in his eyes.

"Come here," Nathan said in a low voice.

She'd heard him say those words before, but usually in a different context. This time, the intensity in his gaze made her heart race. She walked slowly forward and stopped right in front of him. Her finger traced the scar on his right side where the bullet had entered his body, a reminder that he'd been willing to make the ultimate sacrifice to save her.

For a long time after Sherilyn shot him, Janice couldn't sleep through the night. She woke once or twice with her heart pummeling her chest and a cloak of fear so heavy and oppressive weighing her down that she could hardly breathe. Only when she saw Nathan lying beside her, his chest rising and falling in a deep sleep, did the panic subside.

Then she pressed closer to him, relieved that he was alive and well and that her nightmares weren't real.

"Great job today, if I didn't tell you."

"You told me," Janice said.

"Did I tell you that I love you?"

"Not today."

"Well, I do."

He gazed into her eyes, and she saw all his love and devotion. Not once during the past year had he given her any reason to doubt his feelings for her, and for that, she was eternally grateful. Nathan made her comfortable in their relationship in a way she hadn't been in other relationships. He put her mind at ease. He took care of her. He was her champion and her cheerleader. She couldn't ask for a better man.

"I love you, too."

"I know you love me, but do you trust me?"

"Yes," Janice answered promptly.

"Good."

He reached under the pillow and pulled out a velvet box. Janice's hands flew to her mouth. Though she had been expecting a proposal, her excited reaction was genuine.

Nathan lowered to one knee and gazed up at her, taking her hand in his. "I fell in love with you four years ago and right away realized a future without you is no future at all. It would be nothing but a bland, colorless period of time without you in it. I can't imagine spending my life with anyone else but you. Janice, will you marry me?"

Lips trembling, Janice nodded vigorously. "Yes," she said.

A sexy, dimpled smile was her reward. Nathan placed the

emerald cut diamond ring on her finger, and as tears came to her eyes, he stood and pulled her into his arms.

He kissed the corner of her mouth. "You and me, forever," he whispered.

That word no longer scared her. "Forever and ever," Janice whispered back.

Then they sealed their forever with a kiss.

Unparalleled Love series

Did you enjoy this book? Leave a review to let other readers know your thoughts.

And by the way, you'll be able to read more about The Heir, Nina Winthrop, in *Deeper Than Love* (Brooks Family #6), when she reconnects with Reese Brooks, who is determined that she won't get away again.

Until then, read the other books in the Unparalleled Love series!

SOUL'S DESIRE by Sharon C. Cooper. Life is looking up for Soul Carrington, especially when she comes face to face with a past love.

EVERLASTING DESIRE by Stephanie Nicole Norris. The answer to Jada Wilson's quandary comes from an unanticipated source—her best friend.

ALSO BY DELANEY DIAMOND

Brooks Family series

- A Passionate Love
- Passion Rekindled
- Do Over
- Wild Thoughts
- Two Nights in Paris

Johnson Family series

- Unforgettable
- Perfect
- Just Friends
- The Rules
- Good Behavior

Royal Brides

- Princess of Zamibia
- Princess of Estoria

Love Unexpected series

- The Blind Date
- The Wrong Man
- An Unexpected Attraction
- The Right Time
- One of the Guys
- That Time in Venice

Latin Men series

- The Arrangement
- Fight for Love
- Private Acts
- The Ultimate Merger
- Second Chances
- More Than a Mistress
- Undeniable
- Hot Latin Men: Vol. I (print anthology)
- Hot Latin Men: Vol. II (print anthology)

Hawthorne Family series

- The Temptation of a Good Man
- A Hard Man to Love
- Here Comes Trouble
- For Better or Worse
- Hawthorne Family Series: Vol. I (print anthology)
- Hawthorne Family Series: Vol. II (print anthology)

Bailar series (sweet/clean romance)

- Worth Waiting For

Stand Alones

- Still in Love
- Subordinate Position
- Heartbreak in Rio
- Heart's Desire

Other

- Audiobooks
- Free Stories

ABOUT THE AUTHOR

Delaney Diamond is the USA Today Bestselling Author of sweet, sensual, passionate romance novels. Originally from the U.S. Virgin Islands, she now lives in Atlanta, Georgia. She reads romance novels, mysteries, thrillers, and a fair amount of nonfiction. When she's not busy reading or writing, she's in the kitchen trying out new recipes, dining at one of her favorite restaurants, or traveling to an interesting locale.

Enjoy free reads and the first chapter of all her novels on her website. Join her mailing list to get sneak peeks, notices of sale prices, and find out about new releases.

Join her mailing list
www.delaneydiamond.com

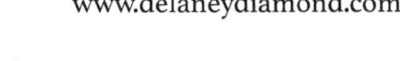 facebook.com/DelaneyDiamond

twitter.com/DelaneyDiamond

 pinterest.com/DelaneyDiamond

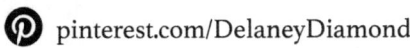 instagram.com/authordelaneydiamond